A Slice of Fear

Short Stories of Suspense

By Andrew Allen Smith

All names, characters, businesses, events, incidents, strange shopping stores, mysterious bookstores, and other stuff in this story are fictional. Any similarity with a person, place, or thing, living, dead, undead, free-floating spirit, vengeful wraith, or other malevolent or protective entity is purely coincidental and the product of a healthy imagination.

ISBN: 978-1-7340960-3-3

LOC: TXu 2-246-752

Contents

Authors Rant

I've always been fascinated by fear. I didn't know how much until I started looking over all the stories I've written and the books I've read over the course of my life. Perhaps it is not fear as a whole that fascinates me but the thrill and excitement of building fear.

I've been in numerous discussions about how fear is good or keeps us from doing something we shouldn't do, but I have never really felt that way. I've always considered fear to be an enemy that should be avoided or eliminated if possible. Still, there's always something that floats around in the back of our minds and finds a way to give us a slight uneasiness or a little faster heartbeat. The grip upon our internal soul has always fascinated me, and it is that grip that sometimes motivates me to write about fear and more.

When I was only six years old, in first grade, the school I went to in Indianapolis played movies each day and let everyone stay and watch. I watched fantastic classics like The Great Train Robbery and other excellent movies in a time where the norm was 16-millimeter film and a speaker played over the PA. One afternoon I stayed and watched "The Blob" and it was at that moment that I first recognized the fear in me. Of course, there were things that made me cautious before that. Still, I clearly remember always thinking of myself as invincible, and after leaving halfway through "The Blob", which I now find to be a very amusing movie, I walked home thinking over and over about how I felt and why I felt it. I didn't really dwell on it as much as I wanted to understand it and it is there that I found my passion for telling scary stories.

It may seem kind of strange that the feeling of fear and overcoming that fear made me want to find that fear over and over again. As I went through childhood, I faced things that no child should ever have to face. Death was at the top of the list, but there was also a series of other items that could have turned me into a very different person. My sister and I faced many of these together, and I look at her and I and wonder how different our lives could have been without many of the obstacles that shaped us.

I faced each of these obstacles and potentially devastating situations with the idea that they were part of a larger whole. This sometimes created situations where I pushed my own envelope and did things that had more than a little danger associated. I didn't always stay in the real world and often daydreamed of different places, different worlds, and different situations that were filled with the threat of fear. Instead of warping me, I found my imagination could create a world that could instill fear in others or at least give them a glimpse of the thrill I once felt and occasionally feel with fantastic storytellers.

As I went through my childhood, I found Alfred Hitchcock and a series of anthologies and other books that made me consider the consistency and purity of fear and the thrill that it can bring. I read a book called "Thrillers and More Thrillers" and found it interesting how varied the stories that people wrote were presented. It was at that point that I started jotting things down. This was the beginning of a series of short stories that would span a considerable time.

Unfortunately, many of those were lost over time, and probably, if not definitely, we're not exactly of the caliber I try to write today. Instead, they were outlets that allowed me to experience a small slice of fear or to face something that I didn't think I could face.

Today I find that I write as an outlet for situations and solutions and that often the fear just comes out. It is not that I set out to write a story about an interaction with the personification of death, but my mind flows that way and suddenly it's there. Sometimes I forcefully take it another direction, but it is just as easy to let go and let the story build itself.

As we spend some time together in this Slice of Fear, remember that it's only a story. Remember that fear is just a feeling, and it is the thrill of fear that sometimes reminds us we're alive or at least gives us the motivation to achieve more. I have found that facing fear can often open up a world of laughter and self-discovery that makes the days a little more fun.

Yes, this is just a rant and I rarely do this in my books but this time I just felt like rambling on for a moment. I really didn't want to throw a bunch of stories out there and have everyone look at them and go "well that was fun" without taking a moment to realize that it was more than a story it was a helping of moments, a thrill of an interaction, and a slice of fear.

Writers Block

I stared at the page.

The darkness and I were old friends, but this was a mockery. The words were screaming in my ears as unintelligible rubbish. Some language I had never studied or heard continued to echo in my mind. No real words came except that small sentence at the top of the page, "The icy hand reached for my heart..."

A few hours ago, I was excited, even elated, with ideas flying through my mind like a sickle in the wheat fields. Oh, what a harvest it would have been. I knew that this would be the story, the play, the book, that would end all books. I had seen the words fly through my mind as though they were not even mine, but they were. There they were, calling to me, and I began to write. Only the first sentence came, "The icy hand reached for my heart..."

After I had written it, the words seemed to jump from branch to branch like some unwieldy spider monkey, reaching for me and then running. I am laughing at the thought of the banana being held to me only to be snatched away as I reach for it. I know the story, I felt it, I heard it in my mind, I saw it in my mind's eye, and the urgency I feel is palpable. Tension is ripping at me inside and out. All I can hear or see or feel now are the words, "The icy hand reached for my heart..."

"Why, why, why," I actually say out loud. I know this, I know this story. I knew it, I know it, I can write it like I have so many hundreds of others. The words can flow from me like water from a fountain, no, like water from a waterfall. I know this, I know it will be fine, I know the words will come and I begin to type. Crazed with the passion of feeling the words flow I begin to type the story. Words fill my screen, and I am feeling good again. The feeling is short-lived as I begin to read my words and find nonsense. Anger fills me as I backspace over all I had just typed and still, the few words remained, chanting to me with near insane gibberish, "The icy hand reached for my heart..."

I took a deep breath, the anxious fervor was calling to me, I knew not how it knew my name, but I felt it there, calling, laughing, even giggling. The silence I so adored was there as well. The simmering words bathed me in their cold embrace as I tried so hard to reach beyond the edge of reason, the edge of my feelings, the edge of that thing inside writers that pushes out the creative talents that so many cannot begin to fathom. Still, I was alone with the words that sat on the screen, "The icy hand reached for my heart..."

I was alone, I felt alone, I could not break this bond that was so strong over me, what was it? Why was I vexed so thoroughly? Why was this massively wonderful mystery of a story before my eyes but unable to talk or call to me? Why was I being punished? I felt my anger well up to the extreme levels near madness. "I am done!", I screamed knowing no one could hear my voice, "Just take it". I sighed, closed my eyes and as the darkness closed in, I heard the voice whisper, "The icy hand reached for my heart..."

"Max, the coroner wants to see you, something about that writer thing," the suited patrolman said.

"Sure," Max replied chomping on the edge of a two-day old donut. Coffee in hand he walked the stairs down three floors to the basement. The lights seemed dimmer here even though they were the same on every floor. Max had been here more times than he could easily count, still, it was a necessity of the job. The stainless-steel door rolled open as he pushed on it. The hinges were silent as a quiet night in the snow.

"What's up?" Max asked the ashen faced bald man hovering over yet another body. "That the guy? Smirking?"

“The writer, yes,” Stan Herks replied. Stan was one of those men who was timeless. No way to tell how old they were. Stan could have been 20 or 70, it just was one of those things.

“Yeah, so, open and shut case,” Max laughed as he took another bite of his stale donut. “What did you need?”

“Well,” Stan began, “It sure isn’t as open and shut as I thought. This was routine. You know we were not sure of a cause of death. He was just dead. A man in his shape. It’s like in his books, you know he wrote mostly mysteries and thrillers? The detectives and sleuths are never sure why the victim would have died.” Stan paused, “I was stumped. After all, he is 42, a little overweight but no family history, he should sit up right now and walk away. At least I thought that until I looked closer.”

“OK, so, I got too many cases and Halloween is coming up, why are you making it harder than it should be?”

“Look at this,” Stan said removing the carefully cut breastplate from the man’s chest. Inside there were lungs and the outline of other organs. They surrounded a gaping hole.

“What is this? I can see there’s something missing?” Max said as he looked on, “Is this a joke or something?”

“No, no joke. His heart is missing. Stranger yet there was no blood. It looks like every connection to his heart was frozen shut as it was removed, but he had no scar. Not even a mark. There was nothing when I opened him up, his heart was just gone.”

Max turned a little ashen, “Like it was frozen you said?”

“Yeah, I have never seen anything like this,” Max was shaking a little. He walked to the wall phone, hit speaker and a button to the side.

“Carson here,” came the voice.

"Yeah, Jim, Uh, what was it that was on that writer guys computer. You know, it had some words on it when we found him."

"Really?" Carson asked.

"Yeah," Max said, "Can you look it up, I just need to know."

"Don't have to," Carson replied, "Was the creepiest thing I ever read. It said, "The icy hand reached for my heart....""

The Bookstore

I stood in the atrium of a bookstore. I was a little muddled and I reached to my face and it was wet, no, more than wet, it was damp and soaked at the same time. I shook my head and heard the voice.

"Sir, are you ok?" the tall man in the crisp black suit said to me, "I haven't seen lightning hit that close in a while. Wow, would you look at the storm."

I turned, outside the door a few feet behind me a storm raged that could only be considered a monsoon. The rain pelted off the door and clinks of small ice pellets jingled like an insane tambourine staccato that held no real pattern. I paused trying to remember something that was almost there, but I could not.

"How did I get here?" I asked the man. He was tall, well over 6 foot and much taller than my 5'11. He was not big nor small and there was a radiance about him, something that imposed control and noted power. Even though I did not feel intimidated I could not remember why I was here, nor how I got here.

"You walked in the door of course." There was a clap of thunder that ripped the heavens in pieces, and I looked outside as a tree fell across the road. "I guess we will be stuck here for a while," he said. "I will make a few calls and see if we can get that tree gone. So how can I help you?"

"I am not sure," I said and looked around the small store. To my left a stage was placed with eerie precision. Couches and tables were scattered around the stage and a bar behind them to the left of the store. To the right there were books, books everywhere of seemingly every type.

"Well, we have a little bit of everything, from the positive to the negative, from the enlightened to the macabre, from history to fiction we have it all. If you can't find what you need, we will find a way to get it for you, all you have to do is ask," the man said. "By the way, my name is Luke. They call me lucky Luke, but my luck hasn't been all that great, it is just so-so."

"Umm, hi Luke, my name is Rob, Rob Pelican. You know, maybe I should go," I said wiping my face dry, "I really don't know why I am here."

"Must be either to get a book or meet someone," Luke laughed, "but you won't be going anywhere until the storm slows down. Why don't you look around and maybe you will remember something?"

I looked back at the door and watched the storm rage. I wiped my face and noted my pants and shirt were mostly dry. I wondered how I had avoided being soaked but did not worry about it now. I started to walk as Luke walked to the back.

"I am going to go downstairs to the office, I will be a few minutes. Look around, I will be right back. There is another customer in here somewhere. Just wait for me if you remember what you were looking for, I won't be long."

I smiled and yelled back, "OK, I will do that." Then I began to walk in the deep stacks of books. Luke was right. If you had an imagination it would be fueled by everything in this store. I wandered through the children's books for a moment, then the teen, books were stacked nearly 20 feet high with sliding mahogany ladders allowing you to climb up. I thought about lawsuits but saw a little gold chain with a sign on the ladder that said, "If you enter the steps, abandon all hope of lawsuit, it is your choice". I laughed at the language and knew it was a literary mention, but I did not know or remember for what.

My head began to feel a little better as I reached the edges of the teen books and entered the romance section. I still did not remember how I got there or why, but I was actually starting to enjoy looking at the books. I saw a book called Q and picked it up for a moment, it was for a young person and I set it down and went on. Further a book called "The Rejects of Room 5" sparked my attention as I had always felt like a reject. Still, it was not what I was there for, so I continued on. I moved into history and historical fiction. A book called "Road Home" was enticing but it was not why I was there.

I turned a small corner and pushed a ladder a few feet and saw a woman looking at books to my right. From where I stood, she was small and well dressed. Her crisp pencil skirt was offset by a lined blouse and a stunning vest. Her long red hair seemed to flow even though there was no wind in the building. She stood maybe 5'7 but 4 inches of that were the stylish black heels and though she wore no stockings her legs were well toned and tanned. That hair, it was haunting until she turned.

"Rob?" she said to me as she looked into my eyes with a mixture of anger and despair. "What are you doing here?"

"I don't know," I said, "I am trying to remember but I walked in through the storm. What are you doing here? I thought you moved to Paris or New York or something?" Her name was Amy, and we had some history, a very deep history.

"I am visiting friends if it matters at all to you," she said with more than a little anger attached to it, "I just wanted to get a gift for their daughter."

I looked at her, she was stunning as always. "You look amazing."

She shook her head, "That really doesn't mean much to me anymore. Once maybe, but I am not even sure why you are talking to me right now."

I paused and considered, "Why wouldn't I?"

"You sure you want to ask that?" she asked me.

"Yes," I replied, "Why wouldn't I?"

Amy seemed to consider her path for a moment. She was a powerful person in my previous position, but she had left that. She was respected by a significant number of people and I had been a part of her team. "Don't go believing your own press releases," Amy said to me. "I know how you pretend to be so Petey pure heart with people, but I grew up. After your little shot across my bow a lot of people came to me and started filling in the blanks, I had been too blind to see."

"Amy," I said to her, "I am not sure what to say. I know I don't know what you are speaking of."

"Oh please," Amy laughed with fiery indignation in her eyes, "I liked how after you set me aside you told everyone I was the bad guy, I like how when people who knew us as great friends asked you about me and if we were going to get together that you said, what was it 'don't you think I could do better'?"

I remembered, and remember saying it to a few people, I cringed being caught but felt bad about it. "I am sorry Amy; I really didn't know what to say."

"Why not say what I said?" Amy continued, seething with rage, "I told everyone you were exceptional and special and would always be a part of my heart." Amy stopped for a second and the rage changed, she was upset but would not cry, the edge of a tear being held back by her indomitable will. "I told people I respected you and your work. I told people I moved on to do better. Let me see, I was told you said I overstepped, I went too far, everything was one sided, that I was a stalker. I was even told you thought I was leaving you candy on your desk, let me ask you Rob, why would I care? You ripped my heart out and slept with another woman and blamed me for your problems."

Some clarity was coming but this was too fast. How had I forgotten all of this until this moment? I remembered saying a lot of things, but I was trying to save my marriage. I looked into her battered but dry eyes, "I was trying to save my marriage." I stated, "You do remember I was married?"

"I was too," Amy said, "It was you who chased me, you who made me feel special when I was ignored at home. You who spent the time talking to me and more. It was you who set me on my path."

I remembered, and I had told Amy that over and over. Yes, it was wrong, but we were both in such wrong relationships it felt so right. I was at once ashamed and angry for what I had done. "Amy," I said, "I'm sorry."

"Sorry for what?" Amy continued, "Destroying my life or trying to destroy my reputation. I did my homework Rob, after I left several men came forward and said they would have warned me but were afraid of me. It seems everyone feared me but you."

I was torn suddenly, the passion, the excitement, the love. It was all there, yes, I loved her and now here I was divorced and alone. Now I lived in a small apartment trying to get by alone. My wife had divorced me when she found out. I felt my anger flair.

"You called my wife and told her about us, you destroyed my life and my marriage," I said with renewed anger.

Amy laughed hard, and the tears were gone, "I know this will count against me when I stand before the pearly gates, but you are a fool of a fool. I said nothing. A friend called me and asked about you, but I never spoke to your wife."

"She said you told her," I said with more force.

"She did huh?" Amy was almost mocking me, "and poor little Rob did not trust me and just coerced himself into belief. What a joke. I thought you were more intelligent than that. It is a 3rd grade move to trick someone, but she had your number and you fell for it hook line and sinker. I bet you even told her about the other gal, what was here name? Wendy? Clair? Who cares? Rob, I will hurt for a long time because of you, but I am done." Amy put down a book and walked past me towards the door. I smelled her perfume and felt her breeze as she passed. I walked behind her, "Amy, don't go."

She stopped and looked at me, "Why?"

"I miss you," I said to her. "I miss us."

"Well," Amy said, "You tell all your friends the truth, and figure it out for yourself, and maybe we will see if I can talk to you again, then again, maybe not. I will feel my love for you every day of my life, but I likely will not share it with you again."

"Amy," I said again, "there is a storm."

"Story of my life, babe, story of my life."

I walked behind her until we reached the door. The storm raged outside, pelting the door like a thousand rainy bullets. A truck was being battered as it was moving the tree in the road.

"Goodbye, Rob, thanks for ruining another day," Amy said as the tears began to flow. Tears I never saw, tears I ignored. I felt her now like I should have before. Amy turned rapidly and slammed out the door.

I went to follow and felt a hand on my arm. "Mr. Pelican, are you OK?"

"No," I said, "I am not OK." I tried to wrench my arm away, but it was held with a grip far more powerful than I could have guessed. I looked at Luke. He looked different now, more foreboding. I had not noticed his eyes, they were nearly black if not a deep ebony black, and I sat looking into those eyes for a moment. "I messed up, I remember Amy telling me once that all I had to do was ask and we would be together, and I waited. I waited for family, for my girls to grow up, for every excuse in the world, and she waited for me. I think I screwed up."

Luke laughed.

"Why are you laughing?" I said with a little anger.

"You screwed up all right." Luke giggled.

"I need to go after her," I said and as I turned there was no door, just a brick wall where windows and a door had been. I ran to the wall and pushed it and my hands burned hot. The wall was impenetrable to me.

"What is going on here?" I stammered. "What is this place?"

"Just a little store," Luke told me, "Well, it is your store after all. You built that wall as well; it is the wall that keeps others out. You are stuck in one of your well-managed boxes. Every time we talk, you ask this, and every time I tell you." Luke walked around on the finely finished wood floor; his perfectly polished black shoes clicked on the floor as he paced. "I actually enjoy it some, this part, telling you. Don't you remember? Your divorce? The pain? Remember saying 'I want to die every day and finally finding your way to do it? Remember the EMTs, and the blood everywhere, your wrists cut?" Images flashed through my mind, and emotions ran with them. I remembered the despair I felt. I felt as though I had lost everything. The world seemed to crush me, and I felt as though I had no way out, no way but one. I had spiraled into deeper and deeper depression. I made a decision to end it all and did so. The blade had cut deep, and I remembered feeling lightheaded, then darkness, then I opened my eyes here, looking at the storm.

"What is going on?" I demanded.

Luke laughed again, "You haven't figured it out? I am disappointed, I know you are a smart man or were a smart man. I am playing a game with you. You need to understand how your actions made your destiny. Everything you did led to this moment with you and me."

"What about Amy," I asked.

"Amy is still alive, and after you, she built her own little hell; she suffers as much as you do every day. She grieves for herself each night as sunset falls. She is her own nightmare, and she may well avoid seeing me." Luke smiled. "You, on the other hand, get to enjoy my company, well, forever. You get to feel this indescribable feeling over and over."

"No, that's not possible." I said, "I am a good person. I help people. I know I cheated and have not followed a good path, but..."

"Ha," Luke laughed, "I see everything remember? You stab everyone in the back. You talked bad about all your friends to your other friends. Those who stood up for you eventually regretted it.

Even your best friend, who came out of the relationship with Amy, figured it out after you killed yourself. Eventually, they all talk to each other, eventually they know. Sure, Amy was no saint, after all she broke her vows to be with you and someday, she might be here, but you, wow Rob, you are an expert at destroying people. A few thousand years from now, I may give you a job torturing people just to watch and be amused. Your sin was not cheating. Your sin was being you. You denied love. You denied friendship. You destroyed yourself."

"What do you mean," I asked, knowing the answer.

"I mean, it is time to remember," Luke said, and suddenly, I did. I had talked to Amy hundreds, no thousands of times. I remembered them all. Sometimes it went as today, sometimes I was nicer, and it was tender, but it always ended with her leaving. Always I focused on the faults and not the good we had. Always she got angry, and I could not connect with that special part of who we had been. Always she walked out the door, the door I could not walk out of, and always Luke gave me this speech.

I began to cry. No, I began to sob. I saw who I was, and I did not like it. "Why?" I asked, even pleaded. "Why?"

"You already know," Luke said, "You can't seem to learn. You think that your way is the only way. You are lost and cannot see beyond that small pitiful excuse of a person you were to what others are and strive to be. Even as Amy is angered, she still loves you. What about you? You lost that ability if you ever had it. Now here is the fun part. Now it's time to forget."

Luke's voice faded, and I felt a strange dizziness cross over me. I grasped and tried to hang on, but the memory of it all seemed to escape like a butterfly in the wind until it was there no more. I felt muddled for a second, and all the things I was thinking were lost. There was darkness for just a moment, finally, a clap of thunder startled me.

I stood in the atrium of a bookstore. I was a little muddled and I reached to my face, and it was wet, no, more than wet, it was damp. I shook my head and heard the voice.

"Sir, are you ok?" the tall man in the crisp black suit said to me, "I haven't seen lightning hit that close in a while. Wow, would you look at the storm."

I turned. Outside the door a few feet behind me a storm raged that could only be considered a monsoon. The rain pelted off the door, and clinks of small ice pellets jingled like an insane tambourine staccato that held no real pattern. I paused, trying to remember something that was almost there, but I could not.

Prices Slashed

A line was loosely formed outside the new store, "Slashed!" and Gayle Levy was glad to be in it. She had heard the store would be the ultimate fast paced shopping adventure and was fired up to get some great deals.

In reality, Gayle knew she didn't need anything, she just loved the thrill of finding a bargain and had gone out for years on Black Friday to get the deal, not the item. Just a few years ago she had made the news when a group of women fought over the last 4K television at a local chain and she ended up getting it, with a few other women getting black eyes. Fortunately, no charges were filed.

The store in front of her was in an old Wal-Mart, closed from the attacks on retail from online shopping companies that offered low prices and near same day delivery for free. In the new world there was no need to even see someone else, Gayle hated the idea of that, after all, where is the fun in that? Where is that thrill of winning?

Looking around the line had grown since she arrived and over three hundred people were gathered to cram into this new store with more cars pulling up every minute. Men in grey uniforms walked around and handed people small papers.

"What's this?" Gayle asked.

"Contract, no one gets in unless it is signed, allows video access and is a general release of liability." the guard said.

Gayle reached in her purse, got a pen, then filled out and signed the paper. Nothing was stopping her shopping today.

A massive bell sounded. The bell was reminiscent of the bell that rang as horses were let out of the gate at popular racetracks. The doors opened wide and the sign "Slashed" lit up bright blue.

People began to push into the doors as men checked contracts. One by one people were let through as their contracts were checked then slipped into a file folder. Some were stopped to sign or change something, but the line flowed with great vigor. Gayle noticed each contract being fed into a document scanner at the door and whisked off to who knows where. Gayle pressed as hard as anyone as she handed over her signed contract. As they pressed forward, she found herself in a massive white room. People stood impatiently and huge fans blew air downward into the group keeping it from getting hot. A diminutive woman stood on a high podium and began talking.

"Welcome to the future of shopping!" the woman began. "My name is Lizzie, and I will be opening these doors in just a moment so you can compete for the best deals you can get anywhere, online or offline. The rules are simple, you make your best deals by getting the products you want at the best price. If you achieve certain goals, you advance to the next room and get more discounts up to the fourth room where you have the opportunity to get 99% off. To advance to more savings you must get the best deal and be chosen to move to a new level. No one moves forward unless chosen."

There were some groans and some "ahhhs" in the audience.

"Now don't worry," Lizzie continued, "Everyone will walk out of here with a deal, but only the most tenacious people will move on to the challenge rooms and better and better prices! As the doors behind me open you will find your deal, and the prices will be slashed based on you and your ability to make your deal happen."

Gayle was ready and the people around her pushed forward.

"When you hear this sound," a groaning low-pitched horn sounded, "someone has checked out and moved out of the area and is headed home or back to the start."

"When you hear this bell," a ring sounded like the one she had heard previously, "You will know someone is moving on to better prices and more intense competition. Is everyone ready?"

"Yes," came the weak yet nervously excited murmur around the room.

Lizzie strained and took a deep breath, "I asked, is Everyone READY?"

Screams echoed in the room as people cheered "Yes!!!!" and the bell rang.

Gayle was pushed forward with the crowd at first and saw bin upon bin in front of her as the halls began opening in the first rooms. There were about 30 bins of difference sizes filled with merchandise. There seemed to be no rhyme or reason to it. To the left was a door marked cashier, huge men in blue uniforms pocketed the area like massive sentinels looking over a prize, everything else was about the deal. This room was massive and could hold hundreds of shoppers.

Within seconds there was a ring and Gayle could not see what happened. She did see a tall woman escorted to a door marked "2" in front of her. Guards at the door kept anyone else from thinking about going to "2" unescorted.

The bell rang again, and another woman moved forward with several items in hand, then another, and another.

Gayle saw a woman with an armload of merchandise head to the cashier door and she heard the low-pitched moan as the woman went out of the one-way door. People were grabbing things left and right. Gayle saw something in front of her, a name brand purse worth a lot sitting on a table. She grabbed at it as another small woman grabbed it as well. The two pulled and Gayle saw a fire in the small woman's eyes. She decided she was going to get that purse and she turned and as she did, she elbowed the woman in the stomach. Choking, the woman dropped the purse.

The bell rang and a huge man in a blue uniform walked to Gayle and pointed her towards door 2. Escorting her she heard the bell ring again and again. More people made their way to door 2. The door swung open, and Gayle was in a new room. There was Lizzie, standing on a new podium. She began to speak.

"Welcome to level 2 where prices are better than any online location could offer! We offer the best pricing because our backers are interested in you and your shopping habits! Get ready to experience shopping like never before in our Electronics Area! Make sure you get a cart to keep your purchases safe!"

People saw the row of carts and began taking the steel reinforced monstrosities and putting their items in the carts. The carts had grates on them that pulled over the front of the top opening making it difficult to reach in. Gayle got a cart, put the purse in it and pulled on the handle closing the top off with a steel grate. She played with the handle and the grate slid up and down on rubber gliders easily. She saw others playing with the lever that worked the grate, and wondered how cutthroat the prices would be to set this type of cart up.

Guards in orange shirts and blue pants opened the next set of doors and the group of perhaps 50 men and women rushed the next room. Gayle pushed forward and was happy her cart was not one from grocery stores. The wheels and bearings were slick and easy and pivoted so easily they seemed to read her mind. Gayle wound her way through the bins and grabbed a few watches and saw the price was hundreds less than normal. A woman grabbed an Apple Watch from her and threw it in their cart. Gayle was furious but saw another one and grabbed it. She put it in her own cart and began to move on when a man started to reach into her cart for the watch, smiling at her with an obvious disdain. Gayle grabbed the grate lever and pulled hard closing on the man's arm. He winced and began to pull back, but as Gayle allowed a little opening for him to withdraw, he began to reach in again. Gayle jammed the lever hard, and he yelped looking at her with obvious anger. His arm pinned he swung at her with his free arm. Gayle grabbed the lever and slammed it over and over until the man began to tear up and started to pull away. Gayle was not having it and pulled again and again catching the man's hand as he pulled out and seeing bruise and blood as he cradled his arm. As the man backed away from Gayle her eyes glared with righteous indignation.

A guard in an orange shirt came up to the man and escorted him out of the area through the door marked "cashier" and she heard the low groan again. Moments later a guard came to her, and she was concerned she was in trouble, but instead the man escorted her to a door marked "3" on the wall, and for the first time in room 2 the bells sounded.

Gayle and her cart were now in a smaller podium room with Lizzie walking to the podium. A massive woman with a bit of blood on her lip and a few items in her cart joined Gayle. Then a man with mussed hair and a slight limp with a fuller cart. He was followed by a short woman with a blonde ponytail that looked like a soccer mom, she popped her gum with her half full cart and Gayle could see a little blood on her running suit.

Soon about 20 people were in the room and as the door opened Gayle could see more and more people entering room 2. Each time the door opened she could hear the groaning klaxon or the ringing bells, over and over like some massive assembly line of shopping.

Lizzie began talking again. "Welcome to level 3. I have a special gift for all of you in here, a 20% off coupon on your cart so far!" Men in green shirts began passing out the coupons to each person in the room.

"Are you ready for kitchen deals?" Lizzie asked.

The room was filled with nervous energy and everyone in that room screamed. "Yes!!!!!"

The bells rang and everyone, including Gayle ran forward with their carts. Gayle grabbed the Ninja blender and threw it in her cart for a great deal off. There were only a few and another big woman in black spandex grabbed one but was knocked down and kicked as a man took it from her. He put it in his cart and Gayle heard the bell sound. She saw the man escorted to the door marked "4" on the side of the room. The big woman in black spandex stood and grabbed a "Kitchen Aid" mixer and as a smaller woman reached for it swung the box by the handle and knocked the smaller woman reaching for it across the floor. The big woman in black spandex put the mixer in her cart but as the other smaller woman struggled to get up, she also opened her cart and took a bunch of items and moved them over to her waiting cart.

The smaller woman on the floor dove onto her and started swinging. As she did Gayle moved to the big woman's cart and took the Mixer. Opening her cart and putting it in Gayle moved away from that scene. Gayle grabbed a knife block from a display and put it in her cart. She then came to a display of meat tenderizers and grabbed one. A hand was on her shoulder, and she turned to find the big woman in black spandex swinging at her.

"Give me my mixer!" the woman screamed. A little blood dripping from her cut lip.

Gayle swung the meat tenderizer up and smacked the woman in the chin. She felt a crunch and the big woman fell back to the floor. Gayle saw the blood spray and the woman's jaw was now at an odd angle. The guards in green came forward and the bells and groans went off at once. Gayle was escorted one way, the big woman in black spandex another.

"She asked for it," Gayle said but soon realized she was moving to the door marked "4".

A new woman was at a podium with only a few others in the room. The 4 waited together as others were ushered into the room and guards with red shirts wandered around the room offering water bottles to the shoppers.

"Hi," the woman said as ten people were counted in the room. "The 10 of you will now compete in our sporting goods department. The deals are amazing, and before we start our proprietors have given each of you a 50% off coupon for any purchases you have made or will make today. Use it with your 20% coupon and your savings will be stellar!"

A muscular man to Gayle's side said, "We aren't gonna get in no trouble are we, I mean, I know I broke that dude's nose, but he was trying to take my vacuum."

"No, by the terms of the store agreement you are in no trouble," she paused, "In fact it is your tenacious shopping habits that make you the best for room 4. Are you ready?"

The ten screamed an affirmative and Gayle found her heart racing. Seven women and three men entered the room. It was larger than some others, but the tables had fewer items. Gayle noticed there were cameras in the ceiling everywhere. Gayle rushed to a counter and grabbed a tent. As someone walked towards her, she opened her cart, threw in the tent and grabbed the handle of the meat tenderizer. A man reached for her cart, and she swung the hammer at his hand, smashing his fingers. He pulled back and looked at her as she blew air to get her hair off her face and swung at his groin. The man's eyes opened wide and he groaned and fell to the floor writhing.

A big black man saw Gayle take the first man down and opened the disabled shopper's cart and emptied it into his in just seconds. Gayle ran to another table with Gerber machetes on it. She grabbed 4 of the big knives and put them in her cart. A few feet down was a table full of baseball bats and Gayle took a bat, then ducked as a small Asian woman swung one at her. Gayle backed off and moved to another table. The Asian woman hit another woman over the head with the steel baseball bat and pummeled her several times. Gayle thought she saw the woman's head deform a little and blood began to pool under her. The Asian woman then took items from that woman's cart.

Gayle looked back at the floor and saw the twisted body of the woman just beaten with the bat. She was now convulsing, and blood was running from a gash in her head.

Gayle moved on to the next table and scraped the contents into her cart with a sweeping arm. She had no idea what she just got but didn't care, it was hers. A dozen boxes filled her cart and as she closed the top grate, she saw she had just taken shotgun shells.

She moved to the next table and turned to see people losing interest in the sales and instead fighting like crazed lunatics over the previous items. As another person fell, the guards in red shirts picked them up and carried them out of the room through the door marked "Cashier". The groan sounds came one after another. The number of people was reduced.

Gayle looked forward and saw the next table and grabbed the item on the table. She knew it well. A Remington 12-gauge shotgun. Gayle reached into her cart, ripped open a box of shells and loaded the weapon with 5 shots. No guard moved, no one came towards her.

Four people remained and Gayle walked back within a few feet of them all. Each was lost in their own fight. Gayle chambered a round as one man looked at her. Gayle shot him in the chest and blood sprayed as he was thrown back. Gayle's ears rang, but she was already chambering a second round and let it loose on the woman to her right. The shot caught the woman's arm and removed it. The woman fell to the floor writhing. Gayle’s heart pounded but she would not lose!

Another woman was running toward the cashier door with her cart and Gayle let loose a third round into her back. Gayle's heart pounded even faster but this was now her deal. The woman's back peppered with blood and she fell forward into the ground. The last man, the black man who had emptied the cart earlier looked into Gayle's eyes. He stood for a moment and pushed his cart towards her, then walked to the cashier door empty handed.

Gayle panted, she walked forward and yelled, "Hey!"

The man turned and Gayle shoved his cart to him. The man smiled and pushed the cart out the cashier door. The groan sounded.

The men in red shirts were cleaning up and taking the fallen shoppers out of the room as Gayle gathered the carts together and moved items to her cart. A few men in black uniforms rushed in with mops and cleaned the floors even as Gayle finished loading her cart. She looked up at the dozens of cameras. Men in grey uniforms came in and were patching walls and painting with rapid haste now. It was a theater of efficiency.

"I'm ready to check out," Gayle said.

Lizzie walked in the room, "Of course Gayle, and the proprietors have given you this special coupon for 99% off for your fantastic shopping ability! Thank you for your tenacity! You can combine it with your other coupons making your days shopping almost free! What do you think!"

Gayle blew the hair out of her face, took the coupon and made her way out the cashier door. "It's a lot better than shopping online!" she replied as she left the fourth room.

Behind the cameras, in another room dozens of men and women laughed. "Good job Mister McMillan. We didn't see that coming. Number 77, Gayle Levy is the winner. She paid 15 to 1. Congratulations sir! The second group is setting up now, place your bets. Only 5 minutes remain until bets are locked for group 2 in the fourth room."

Stoker

Amanda Kramer was excited yet apprehensive about her new job. She was good at what she did. As a business analyst and extreme perfectionist Amanda wanted nothing more than to make sure she exceeded every goal that was laid before her.

The building that she was working in was one that hit the papers over and over. It was a modernized wonder made from an antique wonder. Once a massive power generation station the company she now worked for had stripped it, gutted it, then rebuilt it into an ultra-modern workplace. It wasn't just that they had built this masterpiece, it was that in the process they had kept multiple areas in near perfect historic shape.

Walking into the building she looked up to see impenetrable girders framing a modern set of doors. As she made her way inside and approach the attentive security desk staffed with almost intimidating professionals, she saw the walls in the reception area were of historic brick and those walls set off the modern aspects making it a palace of brick, steel, and glass.

Looking around, the entire area was encased in glass as though she and the security guards talking to her were in a giant fishbowl waiting for a shark to be dropped in with them. She almost felt self-conscious in her black skirt, white cotton shirt with the floral sweater, and her glossy black Prada shoes. She felt overdressed, or maybe under dressed. She just didn't know.

Her morning flew by. She visited HR and was walked around to dozens and dozens of people. Amanda knew she might remember faces but doubted she would remember names. She was walked to a lush office on one of the higher floors that overlooked a city that was being rebuilt and modernized like the building she was in. She could not help but be distracted as the executive explained to her a vision for making technology architecture more resilient. The subtle winding river below her seemed to beckon her to watch and the crisp skyline of the city was not only stunning it kept her mind in a fantastic place that she never knew existed.

As the executive outlined his approach, she gained clarity and realized that she was perfect for this job. Her work in cloud architecture, business continuity, disaster recovery, and highly resilient systems suddenly had her engaged with a passion few in her field could understand. She explained Information Technology approaches on moving to a hybrid cloud and in doing so reducing cost while virtually eliminating the risk that the executive had explained. She was in her element, she was happy. More importantly, the executive was happy.

At the end of her meeting her new supervisor escorted her to the cube that she had been assigned and nodded as Amanda talked. Her supervisor explained to her that she was very impressed with Amanda's resume and her first day interaction was even more impressive.

"We're looking forward to seeing your ideas. When do you think you can have a little something to show us?" her supervisor asked.

"Why don't I put together some preliminary items and we can discuss them tomorrow?" Amanda said.

"You know tonight is Halloween, maybe we should wait and give you a couple of days to get settled in," her supervisor replied.

"That's okay," Amanda said, "I live alone and just moved to the area. No plans for me and nothing that I'm going to do. I'll just stay for a while and get things done."

"We don't want to overwork you on your first day," her supervisor replied with an inviting smile, "but you know you better than any of us what you would like to do. Just let me know how I can help."

Amanda was impressed. None of her previous positions had been as friendly or as excited about her let alone as engaged with her as this one. Most of her previous supervisors had been intimidated by her rapid understanding of situations and then the resolution that she could put together in very short order. Usually, her supervisors we're afraid of her, worried that she was going to try to take their jobs and as such treated her less than favorably, sometimes passively aggressive, sometimes simply aggressive. Today was so different. Everyone she had met was engaged and excited for her to be there.

Amanda worked hard and the day melted away like a chocolate bar in the July sun. Amanda's designs and ideas flowed onto paper and since she hadn't set up her computer at home she continued to work until she noted the sun slowly setting in the western sky.

Amanda stood up and walked to the gigantic western window glancing at the other windows that stood on every wall. The sun was blood red and the walls danced with color from the soon to be night sky. She smiled and watched the sun wink at her as it slowly set. Amanda felt excited and happy and mostly felt at home.

Darkness fell like a 2-ton weight in an old Monty Python show and soon she was bathed in the light only from the overheads. Amanda went back to her seat and continued to work. She was passionate about sharing some ideas, and just kept going, reveling in the feeling of getting things done.

She had no idea when she was finally ready to be done for the evening, she just started to feel a little weary and decided it was time. She didn’t think it was late by any means but as she stood up and stretched and looked around, she realized the view below her was no less than desolate. Even though she was on the second floor and could not see far it looked as though the city had just stopped. She remembered that it was Halloween and guessed the trick-ortreaters were scattered around the suburbs in search of candy and occasional awesome tricks on unsuspecting homeowners. She remembered as a child loving the thrill of Halloween and of course the scary stories and being scared by a holiday. Being scared always felt good and she enjoyed it more than a little.

A noise behind Amanda startled her and she jumped like a cat in an old Loony Tunes cartoon. Turning she found a giant man behind her in overalls and a white shirt. He was almost out of place. His arms looked like bridge cables and his overalls looked faded and worn as though overworked as much as he. His chiseled features were rugged but soft in their own way and his receding hairline had become a ring of hair around a soft balding area at the top of his head. Amanda felt at ease even though she should be intimidated.

“Who are you,” she asked.

“Stoker ma'am, John Stoker.”

“I'm sorry I'm so late I didn't realize how time had flown by. It's my first day and well, I was just trying to make a good impression and get things done,” Amanda said.

“No problem, ma'am,” John said, “I was just walking around making sure everything was safe.”

“What time is it” Amanda asked realizing she hadn't looked at either her watch nor the computer time for hours. “Oh, and I am Amanda.”

“It's almost midnight ma’am and that's when I do my walk around. You never know what's going to happen on Halloween.”

“Well, I was getting ready to leave,” Amanda said, “I could walk with you.”

“Sure ma'am,” Stoker said, “I will happily walk you to the door.”

Amanda gathered her items and put them in a leather tote that she carried with her. It looked almost like a large purse, but it was actually a business satchel where she carried all the things, she felt she might have needed for her new job. She left her laptop knowing that she would be back in just a few hours and then she would present those ideas she had completed this evening.

"May we walk through the old area," John Stoker asked.

Amanda wasn't sure what he was saying but she had noticed the staircase behind the row of desks where she sat, and John walked to the staircase with her following closely behind. She held her satchel and began down the red and tile stairs into another world.

The room at the bottom of the stairs was like a step back in time. The walls were made of the same brick that were by the security desk up front. Across the walls were various displays showing the power plant in different phases of its life. Four bright white lights hung from the ceiling suspended by small cables that gave them a very rugged industrial look. The doors on several walls were different than anywhere else in the building.

The doors were stainless steel or at least looked like stainless steel with brass or bronze fittings making them look inviting and techno like many of the steampunk themes she had seen lately. They were out of place from the glass and steel constructs all over the building and instead these doors looked like portals into time or at least portals to another world.

"These doors are beautiful," Amanda said, "I can't believe they didn't show me these on the tour."

"They usually show them to you on your second or third day, but everyone always finds their way here."

On several sides of the room old brass steam gauges hung showing a slice of the past and how power used to come to be. On one wall newspaper articles were gathered in a large mural and Amanda glanced at those from the distance.

Amanda's watch vibrated. She looked down and realized that it was now midnight. On queue there was suddenly a buzzing and as she moved towards John, she observed that the one set of doors was glowing. The stainless-steel door seemed to have a life of its own and pulsed red and gold and powerful yellowish hews. Amanda could feel the heat emanating from the door as John stepped in front of her.

"I need to get you out of here," John said and started backing away from the doors.

The doors began to swell, and Amanda looked on in astonished horror as the lock melted and the door swung wide. Behind the double doors figures started emerging. These were not figures of men, but instead human-like figures made of molten flame. Where eyes and a mouth should have been was bright yellow and the flaming creatures lifted their arms and pointed towards John and Amanda.

"Ma'am we need to leave," John Stoker said, "we need to leave right now."

Amanda was stunned but John's massive body pushed her backwards as he began backing up from the fiery figures. A short hallway was to their side and John guided her towards a set of double doors. They both bolted through the double doors, but they could still see the flames on the other side.

"What are those things?" Amanda gasped.

"Ma'am it is midnight on Halloween. Those are the ghosts of the people who put their heart and soul into this building, literally."

"What do they want?" Amanda asked with an incredulous tone.

“Well ma'am that's hard to say. After all they are ghosts, but I would say they just are drawn to the light on these few minutes of this special day, specifically to the light of the living.”

John went around the corner, and it was like a small winding maze for a moment. Behind them they felt the heat and the doors suddenly flung open and the molten men came into view.

Another set of doors allowed John and Amanda to move into a long hallway. Amanda remembered this hallway from a tour earlier in the day. It went all the way down to the cafeteria area and the main entrance and exit. As Amanda looked down the long desolate hallway John began to hurry her along.

The flaming men came into view walking in no particular hurry behind them. Amanda noticed as they walked each step left a fiery footprint in the carpet. Listening she could hear the sizzle of the plastic or fiber that was in that carpet as it was melting to the floor.

“We have to hurry ma'am,” John said, “we don't have much time.”

Amanda began jogging with John down the hallway which seemed much much longer than earlier in the day.

She tripped.

"Damnit," Amanda said as she struggled back to her feet. "Even in the heat of the moment I am still a klutz."

John reached down and helped her up as one of the fiery men reached for her. He did not grab her but was close enough and she grabbed her arm as the hair and skin darkened and burnt. The two began a run again as the flaming pursuit resumed and lumbered towards them.

John and Amanda reached the glass doors to the security reception area, and she fumbled with the door, her arm smarting with the burn. The flaming men were now on tile, and each seemed to sink into the tile with each step. John pushed the door open as they closed in, and Amanda screamed. She could feel the heat from them like some bad fire pit was closing in on her and John threw her into the lobby and closed the door behind her. She turned and saw John grab the fiery men and hold them from the door even as he too burst into flames. John held them fast and the doors glowed white hot, the glass bowing in the heat.

Amanda turned onto her stomach then glanced back and closed her eyes screaming. As she lifted her body up, she felt sheets beneath her. The room was in her new apartment, she was still dressed in her black skirt and white cotton shirt with the floral sweater. She lay atop of her bed which was still made. Looking to the side she saw her leather bag on a small divan, the leather contrasting with the crisp silk fabric.

The room was lit by a small lamp, and there were no flaming men, no John, just her and her new apartment.

She looked at her watch, it was 1:00 AM. She looked down at her arm, it was not burnt, but it did tingle with some type of residual energy. Amanda wondered if she had just been part of a bad dream but did not remember getting home or turning on the light. She thought of John, and wondered if he was ok, then chided herself at thinking of a figment of her imagination. Amanda rolled over and fell fast asleep.

The next morning, she came into the office and walked by the security desk. She showed her blue badge to the guard, and they smiled at her. She walked to the door that had blown up in her dream, scanned her badge and walked in. The hall was intact, no fiery footprints or scorched tile was there. The hall was long, but not insurmountable and she walked down it wondering if the small museum area was a dream as well. She navigated through the winding hallway and it was there, like last night, the doors stood like silent sentinels, steel and brass protecting the room. Hiding nothing but the other side of the door.

She looked at the walls, and near the stairs she now knew would lead her to her desk she saw the picture. Men who had supported this building in the before time, and there he was, unmistakable. Near the back row stood a mountain of a man from some 70 years prior, she studied the picture, fascinated and smiled to herself for a moment. Halloween had new meaning for her as there on the back row it was unmistakable. There was John Stoker.

Safe

Molly was alone again.

Although Molly was only 8 years old, she liked being alone in their big house. It made her smile to walk up and down the long hallways between the two wings, and she laughed when she was home alone and could enjoy the thrill of sliding down the long spiral banister from the second floor to the first. Her parents said it was dangerous, but she loved the thrill of the ride down, and because the banister sloped at the end she could slide to the floor and laugh.

The first time she had slid down she had fallen on her bottom. Not wanting to draw attention she walked briskly for a few days even though her bottom hurt a lot. It went away, and she practiced until she knew just when to slow down, and just when to stop so she wouldn't fall. She had not fallen again.

As she explored the old house her father had inherited from a grandparent she became fascinated with all the toys all over the house. There were dolls, and stuffed animals, trains, toy soldiers, and a multitude of other items that glistened, sparkled and made noise so well that she just had to play with them.

It was in one of the rooms that she had found Shelly. Well, she called the doll Shelly, but she really didn't know her name. The doll was old, beat up, and well loved. It wore a simple plain red skirt and a white shirt worn with age. She had on tights with a small rip over her knee, and black patent shoes. A small red necklace dangled from her neck with a heart on it. When she had found Shelly she was under a bed in one of the upstairs back bedrooms, and as she held the doll, she just felt safe.

Shelly had become her favorite companion, and as she walked from place to place, she carried Shelly everywhere. Shelly was never far from her side, and they had great fun sliding down the stairs together. So here again, they were alone, and Molly and Shelly were having a great time.

"We will have so much fun tonight," Molly said to the doll. Mommy and Daddy are gone again, and we can do whatever we want.

It was a fun night already, and Molly and Shelly began running the halls from room to room, snooping like two sleuths. Molly's imagination ran wild, and her long curly golden hair bounced on her shoulders and she laughed with the little doll. Molly was good at being alone.

A sound shattered the evening from the lower floors and Molly was startled but curious. She ran to the stairs and with graceful ease took the banister down a floor and landed quietly on the floor. Lost in the moment Molly raised her arms in a brief gymnast pose but then remembered her reason for coming downstairs.

Molly heard the crinkle of glass and held Shelly close to her as she crept closer, closer, until there, in front of her, two men coming in the foyer window.

The men were dressed in black, and both were normal sized, much smaller than her dad, but they looked mean. One was gruffy with blonde hair and skin so white Molly wondered if he had ever been in the sun. The other was very dark, almost black as night. They both had on black hats as well, like they were trying to be part of the darkness.

Molly ran back to the stairs and ran up them quickly. As she reached the top stair she turned and saw the two men at the bottom of the stairs.

"It's OK little girl, we just wanna get something your daddy owes us, why don't you come down here," the very white man asked.

"No," Molly said and ran into the hallway upstairs hearing the men running the stairs behind her.

She was in one of the bigger bedrooms and looking for a way out and set Shelly on the floor as she tried a duct. No luck. As she reached back to grab the doll someone grabbed her hand.

Molly looked and a little girl was holding her hand. "This way." The little girl said and lead Molly to a wall. Touching the wall in the edge of the molding, a small door opened up. It looked like a wall, but it wasn't. The little girl led Molly into the wall and closed the doorway behind them.

There was a dim light in this little area and Molly looked up to see a vent above her. The room was long and narrow, and turned and she wondered if it went anywhere. She started to move but the little girl softly grabbed her hand and put her finger to her lips. "Shhhh" she whispered.

Molly understood and waited as she heard footsteps crashing around the room. They were obviously furiously looking for Molly, to no avail.

Molly waited, and the sounds disappeared. The little girl smiled in the darkness. "We can go now." She said and opened the door into the room.

"Who are you?" Molly asked.

The little girl in the red skirt and white tights giggled. "Shelly you silly."

Molly gaped, "Shelly?"

Molly looked at the girl and the white shirt, the locket with the heart, the white tights, and light brown hair, it was all there, but how could this be Shelly?

Shelly led them to the edge of the room where they heard the men going through one of the other bedrooms.

"Race you," Shelly said.

The two ran suddenly to the stairs and Molly was determined to win. She grabbed the banister and swung her leg over, then slid down quickly. Shelly had done the same and was right in front of her, well, in front of her was right, but they were both going down the stairs backwards quickly.

"There's two of em," they heard the voices as they reached the top of the stairs.

The two men bounded down the stairs as Shelly and Molly rode the long banister. Molly was going faster and had to make the landing work. As she hit the end, she pushed out her legs so she would not fall but tumbled over instead. She felt dizzy from the fall and saw Shelly land standing at the bottom of the stairs. The two men rushed for Shelly as they reached the first floor and Molly felt dizzy.

Shelly grew and grew, and a full-grown woman stood before the two men, and then Molly thought that woman reached for the men. Her hands were bone and ice. The darkness in the room seemed to seep in from the shadows and surround the woman as the two men tried to run. Their legs were frozen in place, and they looked at the woman in horror. The men screamed for a moment as the shadows left the woman and seemed to surround the men now, the room was cold for a moment and the two men began to shake and shimmy like butter in a frying pan. The two men then fell to the ground, but neither looked the same. Their eyes were no longer looking at the room, but lost in something else, some scene only they could see, a scene they might never escape. Molly looked back up, but the woman was gone now, and the little girl Shelly was gone now too.

Molly shook her head and walked towards the two men and saw her doll laying on the floor. She picked her up and ran to the door just as her mother and father walked in. Molly yipped a little.

"What is going on here, what happened to the window?" her father asked.

Molly turned and looked at the men, spasming on the floor.

"What on earth," Molly's mother asked.

Molly just held her doll close and knew she was safe, safe from anything that could come for her.

Broke Down

“Damn this car,” Jean said as she lifted the hood of the nearly antique Toyota Camry.

The area was quiet, desolate and only the crickets heard her as she looked under the hood in the twilight of the newborn night.

“What the hell am I doing?” Jean said to herself as she looked at the car, “I wouldn’t know what to do even if I knew what was wrong. Why is it I always get the bad cars?”

Jean sighed, and stared at the engine compartment, the hood light’s glare shining over all it could see.

Jean picked up her phone and looked at the screen, “no signal”.

Jean began walking back and forth on this desolate part of the highway, looking for a small place that she could get a signal and make a call to someone somewhere.

She saw the lights in the distance, the area she thought no one would ever visit was being visited, she looked at the lights as they grew, from yellow to bright white as the car came closer and she waved her arms.

The car pulled towards her as the last vestiges of the crimson sky faded to black and night was upon the area. The sleek Impala was jet black, and the door opened in an almost methodical manner.

A mountain of a man stepped out of the car. He was at least six feet tall and was very heavy, at least 300 pounds. Jean gulped for a second as he looked at her then he spoke with a soft voice that simply did not fit his mountainous form.

“What seems to be the problem?” he asked.

"Car broke down and I've got no signal," Jean smiled her biggest brightest smile. "I can send a truck for it later, can you just take me to town?"

"Town's about 20 miles from here," the crisp voice replied. "I can take ya, but I am not sure what's open, and there isn't good cell signal anywhere in the state as far as I know."

"So I have found out," Jean said to him, "My name's Jean."

"My name's Miller," the man mountain spoke in a soft tone, "I will drive ya so you can get a signal."

"Thanks Miller," Jean said as she walked to the Camry. "Let me grab my bag."

Jean grabbed the large leather bag out of the back seat of the Camry and walked to Miller's Impala. As she walked to the passenger side she smiled at the crisp lines of the car.

"What year?" she asked Miller.

"1996," Miller said, "A nice year for Impala's. Did you want to lock your car or close the hood?"

"Naw, maybe someone will steal it," she laughed.

Miller looked serious, "I doubt it Miss Jean, people out here are pretty trusting and trustworthy."

"I've noticed that," Jean said as they both closed their doors and Miller started the car.

As they pulled away Miller asked, "So whatcha doin out this way?"

Jean smiled and even in the dark she knew her smile could be seen, "Well, I am kinda looking for something exciting. I am not sure what yet, but there is something out here."

"I imagine so," Miller said. "From the city?"

"Yep," Jean started, "I am from just outside of Chicago, ever been there?"

"No ma'am," Miller said in his light voice, "I've never been anywhere but here. I just work and come home every day like the good lord says to do."

"Family?" Jean asked.

"I did have, but they are all gone now, it is just me and the cat, ain't no issue though, the cat is outside til I get home, and I just work when I want, it is a perfect life." Miller said.

"I bet it is," Jean said. Jean loosened her hold on her bag and smiled a bit. As she did so Miller asked quietly, "that's a nice bag."

"Yeah, I picked it up a bit ago, it is a nice bag," Jean said as she reached into her bag.

"Hey Miller, I am feeling a little sick, can you pull over for a second, I am not used to riding passenger," Jean said.

Miller frowned in the dim glow of the instrument lights, "Sure." He said in his soft voice.

Jean opened the door with her bag as she stepped out of the car and leaned over the side coughing, Miller came around the back of the car and tried to help as she looked down into the ditch and coughed again.

"Can I help you ma'am?" Miller asked.

"You already did," Jean said as she swung the knife across Millers throat.

Miller gasped as his skin parted and blood began spraying out of the gaping hole. Jean smiled as Miller grabbed his throat.

"You're a nice man Miller," she said, "But I am not a nice woman. I really needed the car, the last guy just didn't take care of his piece of junk, and your car will get me a long, long way. Thank you, Miller." As Jean said the last word, she kicked the giant man into the ditch as he gasped his last breath.

Jean walked to the driver side and looked at her phone, still no signal, what a great state. She got in the car and began to drive, wherever the road might lead, and to whoever she might find next.

Hunted

He ran.

He was panting like a dog as he ran in the vengeful heat. The sun slammed down on him and the thick underbrush snagged his pants as he bounded forward. Tim had woke up in a strange cot in the middle of nowhere. The tent he woke in was stocked with water and food and littered with discarded wrappers and empty bottles from some long-forgotten tenant. As he stepped out of the tent into the jungle, he had seen he was alone, and started calling out.

A gunshot had fired, and that is when he began running. He was not sure why, but he was an easy target for whoever had placed him in the tent. He somehow knew he had to get away, well, it seemed like common sense. So he grabbed a few bottles of water and a little food and then he ran.

After 15 minutes of running, he stopped and surveyed the area. He was in a thick jungle, there were animal sounds everywhere. He knew from the sun position he was running either due east or due west but would know shortly when he figured out if the sun was rising or setting. The cover was thick, some areas of the forest so thick it appeared dark, but the heat and humidity were oppressive, and it was obvious he was still in the tropics.

He thought and tried to remember, he was in Cayman, and the night before, there were drinks, and laughter, and he could barely remember the evening going by, he just woke up and was in the tent. His thoughts were jumbled and confused.

Another shot fired, it seemed farther behind him, but he needed to add more distance, and start doing things right. He walked carefully through the brush and was careful not to catch or bend the leaves. He was methodical and kept moving towards the rising sun. He knew now he was going east. Twice he doubled back upon his steps and changed paths, twice he was sure he left no trail, but wanted to be even more sure.

He became more relaxed, and passed several thickets and noted their locations. When he found one thick enough, he doubled back and worked his way in, then watched and waited. The sun slowly moved up to the late morning sky, and Tim felt a little more at ease, perhaps even safe. The jungle was alive with sounds, and he looked up and watched birds fight in the trees over who knows what.

With a shriek the birds scattered, and Tim heard footsteps in the woods. He strained to hear more but could not. Peering through the trees he saw movement, khaki and green contrasted with the rest of the backdrop and he watched as the shape moved slowly, looking at the ground, then sliding forward, panther like. It was a woman, maybe 25, a long rifle hanging from her back she paid close attention to the ground as she moved forward, then she smiled and looked right, then left. Her red hair was long and flowing, she walked easily, the ground seemed to respond to her as she wandered through the ferns and thick vines.

"I can smell you," she yelled. "You sure drank enough last night, I know you are close, c'mon out."

Tim quietly smelled himself, and there was a light stench of alcohol, but no one could smell that well.

"C'mon Tim," she said, "It was a good night wasn't it. I told you that you might get lucky today, lets go back to the tent and have some fun." She flung her head back and swung her hair. Any other time it would have been an open invitation, but Tim was wary.

Tim could not remember her or the night before. He strained, and still, the night was just a blur.

"Tim, where are you Tim?" she cooed. "We can have another drink. You told me all about your life in the service. It's me, Stephanie, you remember."

Tim was so unsure. He sat patiently and thought of standing and seeing what would happen or waiting and seeing if she really could smell him. He watched her, looking around, then saw her run forward.

It was a ruse. She could not smell him. She was baiting him. Why? Why would she be baiting him? He waited, patiently, and suddenly the sounds of the jungle were back. It was almost noisy compared to a few minutes ago. He stayed, waiting, watching. The birds fought above him. He smiled to himself, took a water bottle out of his pocket, and broke open the seal. He was glad he could know it had not been opened before, but still, he took a tentative taste, nothing. He took only a few sips and reached into his pocket, and grabbed a granola bar. He ripped open the package and took a bite.

"Sound is your enemy," he heard the female voice say behind him. He turned and saw the barrel pointing at him. There was a flash of light, then darkness.

The club was full of men as Stephanie wandered through. Her bright green dress sparkled in the flashing lights. As she walked to the bar, her red hair shining in the white light, a man walked up to her.

"Hey," he said, "Can I buy you a drink?"

"Let me buy you one," Stephanie said as she felt the vial in her necklace and walked to the bar with her next prey.

Alone and Afraid

"Sweetie, are you going to have a good night?" Elizabeth's mother asked softly.

"Sure mom," Elizabeth said looking at her mom in her sharp Madonna costume. The leather was tight and Elizabeth was hopeful she looked as wonderful when she got her mom's age. "You look great!"

Her mom looked down at the outfit and said, "Wow honey, thanks. Not too bad for an old woman."

"Mom," Elizabeth whined, "You aren't old. You are only 35, I know moms that are a lot older than you."

"Thanks honey," her mom said. "I won't be too late."

"Stay out mom," Elizabeth said. "Puffles and I will be fine." The large tortoise shell cat purred at Elizabeth's side and rubbed against her.

Her mom walked to the door, and the door closed leaving Elizabeth alone. She heard the lock motors whir shut from the crisp new electronic lock her mom had bought.

Elizabeth got up from the plush couch with the pillows thrown from side to side and walked to the kitchen. She reached into the new Samsung refrigerator and got a Coke, then walked over to the cabinet and grabbed a box of crackers. She noticed they were almost out, so she said, "Alexa, add Cheez-its to grocery list."

A computerized voice from the Amazon Echo said, "Got it, Cheeze-Its added to your grocery list."

Elizabeth went back out to the couch and turned on the Samsung TV then talked to the remote and said, "Scary movie."

Checking her phone, she saw that Facebook was going crazy with costumes as her friends were out in force, going from spot to spot having fun while she sat at home. She really didn't mind, because it was just as fun watching them get into trouble and her not being in trouble.

A list of movies came up and she quickly choose "A Nightmare on Elm Street" and a good choice to watch. Puffles came to her and laid down next to her leg, and she absently stroked her fur as she sat watching the movie. Cringing at the knives she hugged Puffles and he purred away. He was warm, and she always enjoyed feeling the big fluffy cat next to her. It made her feel safe. She felt the tile on the cat's neck and laughed to herself how they "tracked" the cat.

At a particularly tense point Elizabeth screamed and Puffles jumped from the couch and went to the other room. She picked up her phone again and noticed there were no new posts, nothing at all.

Elizabeth jumped as she heard a "whoomp" and a crash in the kitchen. Getting up she walked to the kitchen and turned on the light. The light flickered for a moment, and she looked at the bulb, but then the light stayed on brightly. She looked around and noticed a small bit of hair on the Samsung refrigerator. On the screen it said, "Cat=Food".

Elizabeth opened the door and Puffles ran out of the fridge shrieking.

Elizabeth ran to him and picked up Puffles, holding him close to her chest, "There there, are you ok? How did you get into that fridge?"

Puffles "meowed" and she walked in circles in front of the TV.

"He wants the cat back," the TV said gruffly with Freddy Krueger's face on the screen. "He wants it back now."

Elizabeth backed away from the TV and held Puffles close.

Looking at the kitchen, only a short distance away she saw that Freddy was on the screen in there too, "Give me back the cat. Maybe we should take you too."

She heard the Echo in the kitchen say, "Elizabeth added to grocery list." and Elizabeth cringed. Grabbing her phone she ran to her room with Puffles.

Looking down at her phone she saw Freddy's face and a smile on it, "You can't get away from us, we are everywhere."

Her Apple computer a few feet away lit up. "Bring us the cat and it will be ok."

She ran from her room to her mom's room. The iPad on the counter lit up, "Bring us the cat. Being a smart Refrigerator makes him hungry." The image of Freddy said.

Elizabeth ran out and ran to the door holding her cat. She started to turn the door lock but it glowed bright blue and closed again, "Bring us the cat. We want the cat." She heard the Echo say in the other room.

A small disc started heading towards her and she realized the Roomba was coming for her and Puffles. She screamed and ran back down the hallway to the living room again. She dove over the Roomba with the cat and curled on the couch with all the fluffy pillows.

The TV lit up with Freddy again, "Give us the cat, now Elizabeth."

She heard chanting from all around, electronics sung in their own unique voices begging for the cat, pleading for the cat and Elizabeth kicked her leg's back and forth on the couch.

She heard "Meeeowr" from her chest and looked down.

Puffles eyes glowed red and gold, the circuits were embedded deep into his head and his fur was like thin wire.

Elizabeth screamed into the pillow.

"Honey," her mom was shaking her. "Wake up honey, you're having a dream.

She looked up and saw her mom in her outfit, a little tussled.

"Mom?" Elizabeth said quizzically.

"It was a good night," her mom said. "You should have watched something besides scary movies, you silly."

Elizabeth shook her head, Puffles lay beside her purring, the pillows surrounded her like a cocoon and she was less afraid than a moment ago. She looked down at her phone, at the TV, and all the technology she had. Sitting it on the coffee table she walked towards her room.

"Mom," she said. "I think I am going to read a book and skip technology tonight.

"Sounds good," her mom said from her room.

Yes, it did sound good, thought Elizabeth.

Weeds

Bobby was walking deep in the woods now. He had been walking for a while and was not sure how far he had gone. What had started as a curiosity had become a personal mission, a mission to find whatever had fallen from the sky.

Only a few hours ago Bobby had been sitting on the back porch of his home playing with fireworks and his new Sparkr lighter outside of Whitehall, Michigan. He laughed at how the electric current lit the fuses so quickly and he threw the M80s on the ground and watched them explode loudly. He had gotten into his dad's workbench and filled a sandwich bag with Pyrodex gunpowder and was going to blow it soon with the lighter but did not know how it would go. Another boom as he threw another M80 to the back yard and Bobby laughed. Bobby wasn't worried about people. His house backed up to the Huron Manistee Forest and the park was more than a little large. He remembered walking in the park in the daylight and how easy it was to get lost, but at night, well, it may well be a fool's errand, so he doubted anyone was behind him.

As Bobby sat and watched the breeze, enjoyed the twilight, and of course threw fireworks occasionally, he had seen the streak in the sky. It descended rapidly and plunged behind the trees somewhere in the park. Moments later he heard the "foom" of a landing somewhere and knew a meteor had hit. Bobby knew that the first to find it might well get some cash, or at least a story in the Grand Rapids paper. Standing he brushed off his cargo jeans, picked up two flashlights on the porch and set off into the woods. Bobby was ready to seek a fortune and maybe a little adventure. He checked the batteries so he would not get stuck in the darkness and grabbed a compass that he had been playing with earlier in the day.

Now hours into his adventure the biggest thing he had discovered is that it was much darker in the woods than he had remembered. At 18, Bobby had gone through these woods on his quad, his cycle, and on foot, but never really past twilight. After all, it would not be out of the question to see a bear in the woods, and some places the ways out were tough to find. Bobby's denim jeans and denim jacket let him walk without having to worry about the weeds and wild thorns that would have cut him if he were unaware.

Bobby thought he should run into Silver Creek Road, or at least a house already and considered he may be turned around. Pulling out a compass he verified he was still heading north towards the sound of the streak and wondered if his adventure and his fortune was lost or worse, someone else got to it first.

Bobby turned off the flashlight for a second and looked up at the stars. His eyes adjusted and the light of the stars was enough to see a little, then more as the sky above him slowly lit with the canopy that many people don't ever get to see. Bobby loved looking at the stars in the country, it made him feel large and small at the same time. He looked out and was again amazed at just how many stars he could see, and for a moment wondered if anything out there was looking up at him, as a point of light in their sky. As he looked back down through the trees, he saw the glow.

It was there in front of him, not far, maybe 25 yards. The glow was weak, and his flashlight probably kept him from seeing the dim golden hue. Bobby squinted and struggled trying to see a little further but could only see the dim golden glow. The brush seemed thicker as Bobby worked his way forward. His leather work boots were perfect for pressing through the thick undergrowth but he had failed to bring gloves, so he paid careful attention to his hands as he pressed on.

15 yards.

10 yards.

Suddenly he was in a clearing. A natural dune rose a few feet in front of him, and there, in the middle of a patch of brush was the glowing rock he had been seeking. Bobby considered he had now found his prize and it was time to cash in.

The meteor was small, only about the size of a cantaloupe, and Bobby looked on in fascination as it seemed to pulse and glow in the night. Looking up he saw the light was too bright for him to see any but the brightest stars, and he suddenly came to the realization, he had brought no gloves, nor shovel nor anything that would make it remotely possible to carry a glowing blob of hot rock back to the house.

He surveyed the area. It was obviously hot, he saw the glass around the crater and knew the dune had melted as the meteor slammed into it, but there was no gaping hole, which was a little confusing. He looked around, and saw no burnt branches, or trees knocked down, only the crater with the glowing rocks on top. Bobby looked back at the mound and saw a series of dandelions forming as he watched, a perfect circle of them around the crater. He knew the plants well as he had played with the weed all his life.

He was fascinated to watch the flowers suddenly grow stalks and bloom in mere moments, the yellow flower was mesmerizing and seemed to pulse as it widened and grew. No ordinary dandelion, the flower began to stretch and was soon over 6 inches wide. Bobby was curious, but he had seen that movie where the meteor made some guy into a plant and then he had to kill himself. He was not stupid, not stupid at all.

Bobby smelled the perfumy smell that seemed to entice him. It was musky but sweet, and it seemed to be all around him. He felt as though he should go to the flower, but his mind screamed inside, no, and he began to back away. As he did so his flashlight played across a reflection, and he saw a deer walking slowly towards the flowers. The deer saw him, was antsy but seemed to be pulled to the flower. As it got within a foot the yellow flower sprang out like a launched missile, and Bobby jumped as the deer struggled to get away, now impaled on the glowing petals of the flower. The flower seemed to close, and Bobby was horrified to see the deer seem to shrink as the stalk bulged and shrunk, the animal being emptied like a Capri sun bag.

Bobby continued to back away slowly, and saw the deer, now a leathery hush, fall away. The golden glow pulsed just a little brighter and the flower pulled back to the small group of fat dandelions. The once closed flower that had just eaten a deer began to open, instead of the yellow flower stalks Bobby saw thousands of white seeds ready to be launched. Bobby remembered as a child picking dandelions and blowing on similar seedlings and watching them spin off into the air. His father had told him long ago, "don't blow them away, they'll spread everywhere." These seemed far more sinister than his childhood memories, far more sinister and, looking at the deer husk, far more deadly.

Suddenly, as if to shake him from his thoughts, Bobby was filled with a newfound purpose. He saw a raccoon slowly make his way forward to the flowers drawn to the scent still assailing his senses. Bobby knew if the seeds caught the air, it would be bad.

Against his fear. Bobby walked closer to the plant while reaching into his pocket. He saw a flower turn slowly to him as he opened the baggie and threw the powder inside all over the little mound. It was not thick, but it was in the flowers and made them glisten with black specks. He had played with this powder often and saw the small piles all over the leaves and flowers, he hoped it would be enough.

He backed away again as the raccoon got closer. Bobby picked up a rock from the ground and threw it at the raccoon, but it scowled at him and curiously moved forward. Bobby reached into his pocket for a lighter and his fireworks. He had 5 M80s left in the front pocket of his pants. Bobby quickly twisted the fuses together, so they were one big fuse, ready to be lit. He had done 2 at once before and blown up a mailbox. Old man Simmons was furious with him, but he had paid him for a new mailbox and the man had calmed down.

Bobby lit the Sparkr and the fuses danced immediately. He threw them right to the center where the meteor still glowed and started to run. In a flash in his mind, he thought about how the pieces might hit him, he thought of his mother, his friends, he even thought about old man Simmons as time seemed to dance around him like a wild dog.

Bobby had not taken three steps when the explosives actually went off. The boom was a series of several, not all at once, but a few at once made it seem massive. He actually seemed to hear a scream and turned to see the flowers on fire with sparks dancing through the air, the gunpowder lit as the flames heated and forced the flames to jump wildly in the air. The white seeds were caught in the heat rising but as they would each begin to rise they burst into flames making small streaks of light like the one bobby had seen cross the sky.

Bobby's ears rang like a pan had been placed on his head and beaten with a wooden spoon. He rubbed his head and smiled. Bobby felt good about himself for a moment, he had done something right. To the side of the plants, he saw the raccoon shake its head as if trying to clear the ringing in its ears and run away, spared the fate of the deer.

Minutes later old man Simmons and the police arrived, they were dubious of his story until they had seen the deer, and they looked at the burnt leaves. The meteor was still there but charred and not glowing. Bobby was taken away from the area and watched as it was surrounded with bright yellow police tape. They took Bobby home, and he sat on his porch once more, looking at the stars and knowing that somewhere out there someone was looking up at him.

As people talked some would say the government came and took everything away, some would say it was all just burnt up, some even said it was all a hoax and nothing really happened, but Bobby always knew, if he hadn't gone in the woods, well, we could have all been in the weeds.

A Conversation with Death

The street was nondescript. It could have been any of dozens of downtowns I had visited, but I knew right away it was downtown Frankfort, KY. The little coffee shop stood as it always did, calling me in with memories of Chai and special moments long since passed. Coffeetree had been a nice place to go for a moment when stresses were high, but it seemed like long ago.

I was not sure how I had gotten here, nor was I sure what I was doing here, but I felt the tug, the call, imploring even demanding I go in, so I did.

The door creaked on rusted old hinges, and I was assailed by cinnamon and coffee smells that grasped onto me and held me tightly. As I looked around the lone worker mopped the floor, seemingly oblivious to me, a dozen feet away to the back of the room sat a man.

He was small in stature from my point of view, wearing white long pants and a yellow shirt, as if a part of an old Miami vice episode. His hair was thinned and balding and he reminded me of the villain from an old Star Trek episode and I half expected to hear "Redjak, Redjak, Redjak" echo in the room. He was smiling at me, and seemed comfortable in the room, oblivious to the worker, but quite focused on me.

I looked around the room and saw no one else.

"Come," the man said, "Sit with me."

I was cautious but curious as I walked to the small wooden table. As I reached him he truly was a small man, slightly pudgy and white, his crystal blue eyes looked into me and seemed to sparkle from blue to green as I considered the moment. I stood at the edge of the table.

"Do I know you?" I asked quietly and glanced at the young woman worker mopping the floor.

"Yes," he said back to me glancing at her, "we are quite intimate friends you and I."

"I have never met you, I don't know you, and I am not sure what's going on, so I think I will go," I said quietly.

"Sit," he retorted loudly then lowered his tone, "Please."

"Why?" I asked somewhat impatiently, pausing looking back at the young woman as she mopped. "I don't know you but you say I do, tell me who you are?"

"It will be difficult for you at first, perhaps not so much as others, but still hard for you to believe me, but sit and let's talk," the little man said with a smile.

I paused, looking first at this queer little man in the yellow short sleeve shirt, then at the girl who had begun cleaning the coffee machines. She was oblivious to us both, and as I looked back at the man and his almost cute smile, I felt no threat and simply said, "for a moment", and sat down opposite him at the table.

The man smiled, "First, you keep looking at the young lady, her name is Wendy. She has been working here for a short time and expects no one to be here. The doors are open, but we are in the "lull" period for her as she prepares to close. It will not matter as she cannot see us, hear us, or even perceive us at all, not even a little."

I smiled, then turned a little, "Really?"

I laughed and yelled, "Hey Wendy!!"

She continued with her work like some deaf slave, not knowing that anything was going on. "Wendy!!!" I yelled again, and nothing.

The little man laughed, "I told you, but I knew you would not believe. You have always tested the truth, even if you were sure it was the truth. You have been that way since your first steps and your first words."

I turned back to him, "Really?" I said incredulously again, "and how would you know that?"

"Simple," the man said, "I have been watching you for a very long time, since before you were born. You have seen me before, and we have had many near run ins where I would meet you more closely, but I always watched you from close or afar."

"Who are you?" I asked with a furled brown more frustrated and curious than anything else.

"Have you not guessed?" the little man asked, "I am Death."

I looked at the little man with his white slacks, the sandals, the yellow finely pressed short sleeve shirt and the bald head slightly shining at me, his pudgy little face smiled at me with a knowing look, the look someone gets when they know something about your mother. I looked him up and down, knowing I would not have given him much thought in a bar as he was not a threat. I finally smiled and said, "Well, thanks for dressing up for me, how is the job going?"

The little man laughed, "Again your skepticism. We need to get past it. So how do I prove this to you?"

"Well, you are not exactly what I expected, I mean, the yellow shirt is cool but…" I started.

The room seemed darker as the life seemed to be drawn from everything around us. As I watched the little man burst with what could only be described as the depths of black and folds and cloaks formed around him as he grew closing in on the ceiling, the pudgy little face was replaced with a Cheshire grin from a polished skull dripping with seething energy. His eyes went from crystal blue to ebony flames that flickered in a light from someone inside of him, and in the folds of his now heavy cloaks appeared a blade that could only be considered awe inspiring, the edge dripped of an edge that cold slice atoms, and it seemed to glimmer in both light and darkness. I heard his voice come from the near white skull, "I find this to be a little more intimidating when meeting people, so I try to avoid it. It also makes it hard to order coffee."

"I could see that," I said with a smile, "Maybe you should try a yellow cloak."

As he laughed there were flames flowing from his nostrils and I watched the process reverse until the small man sat across from me again. "Still the humor, I knew you would not be afraid."

"If you wanted me dead, I am assuming I would be dead right now," I said.

"Well, it doesn't always work that way," the little man looked down at the table, "and that is partially why I am here."

I was instantly attentive. After all, whether true or not, this seemed real. Behind me the girl continued cleaning and I noticed a customer walk in with the door creaking. They began talking and I looked back at my pseudo host in his yellow shirt pressed so perfectly as he began talking.

"You see Andrew, we should not be talking," he began, "I mean, you should never have been born. You have heard the story from your mother that she was told she would never have children, well, it was true, but somehow the lineage that you were attached to bonded, and you found a way. There is no way you could have lived in the split uterus, but you did. No way you could have been born in the time you were born, but somehow you came out alive. I was there waiting to take you, and you came out like a long piece of spaghetti, and as I waited, you fought for life. Even just born you fought and began crying and fighting for your life."

I looked at him and shifted slightly as I heard a steamer running in the background, the man who had walked in was getting his drink made. I focused intently, "Well it was not a perfect birth I heard, but I don't remember."

Leaning forward he touched my head in the center and for a brief moment I saw it, I felt it, the struggle through the clamps as I was pulled out of the c-section. The pain was agonizing, and still, I felt pain as the doctor spanked me, and I began crying. I also felt inside me a want, a need to be alive. Death leaned back, and I was looking at him wide-eyed, "wow." I said quietly, "That was cool."

Death laughed for a moment, "I have only done that a few times and usually people scream and pass out, leave it to you to think it was cool."

"Why all the pain?" I asked.

"You have been in pain your entire life," Death began, and I nodded, "I know because I put it there. I wanted you to know that I was still out here waiting. It is funny, I thought eventually the pain would do its work, but you have even managed to adapt to that."

"I still feel it all the time," I said, "Why didn't you just go?"

He chuckled again and continued. "I did not have time to stay too long as there are a multitude of things going on across the universes, but I stayed aware and as your mother became aware of you, I knew your life would be interesting. I visited often over the first few months, and you grew so fast, you were a lazy eater, but you ate well. I was still frustrated as you should not have been, so I visited again a little over a year later. To me it was an instant, but you had grown. You sat on the pew in the church, and it was me in front of you, you saw me, and I thought I could fix this problem with that advantage, so I beckoned you forward and you toppled off the pew, but that hard head of yours was a little too hard. You barely cried as they rushed you to the doctor and put in stitches. Again, I was frustrated by your very existence."

I heard the door creek again as the customer left, the young lady again furiously cleaning as darkness seemed to grasp at the day.

"Sorry about that," I grinned a little as I turned to Death, "Is this whole thing to take me away now?"

"No, we will get to that," Death said with a slight nod, "I came for you again just a few years later, you were playing out front of your trailer. I told you the pot needed to be turned back over, whispered it to you and you , as a child, pulled that cast iron pot down that by all accounts you should not have been able to move, and it missed you by going between your toes, more stitches, but still you were here and should not have been."

"OK," I said, "I remember that, but I don't remember you whispering."

"Oh, I am subtle like that, my whispers often come in random thoughts and ideas," he smiled, "and are not always as words."

"Makes sense, so how did I resist that time?" I asked.

"You didn't, but blind luck saved you. Another year passed and I grew more frustrated. I tried to set up situations that would lead to your demise. When your father was tempted and left, I thought I had my chance." He spoke.

"The car, right?" I asked.

"Yes, it was perfect, your mother had set it up for me. You wanted to do what was right, and continued to have the heart of a righteous warrior, and when the car hit you, I thought this would finally be over." Death said in a rather annoyed voice.

"Hard head again," I said dryly.

Death nodded, "Hard head, no one's head is that hard. You were hit by a car, thrown 25 feet, I smiled as the people gasped in horror and you tried to get up. You walked away with two bumps on your head. I was frustrated beyond compare." Death said in an annoyed tone, and I noticed his eyes were no longer the crystal blue, but more black.

"You ok?" I asked.

Death shook his head a moment and his blue eyes returned. "Only you would ask Death if he was ok."

I laughed, "Well, I wouldn't want you to die or anything."

We both laughed hard.

"It was after the car that I realized that you made me laugh. It became a game between you and me, and I knew time was on my side." Death stated still smiling.

"Yeah, I bet you live a little longer than me," I said smiling.

"I have lived a million million million of your lifetimes and more. It would be hard for you to understand as time is not a true measure, but it is the only way you can comprehend the world." Death said stoically.

"I understand some, simultaneous time makes sense to me, and I have considered it over and over," I said.

“If it were that simple, but for now, it is good,” he started, “You need to know that all the things I did, I did almost as a game. There was no malice. You should not have been alive. I tried one more time with a passion.”

I looked at the table, “The riot.”

“Yes,” Death said, “humans are so predictable, and I set up your school to be polarized against whites, you were the minority. When your friend was killed it was supposed to be you.”

“I remember,” I considered for a moment. The mass of hundreds of black students and men in an elementary school, the gangs, and us running for the door to be safe, I was pulled in as Brent’s head was smashed into a wall. My gym teacher shot, and people were hurt, including teachers and officers. It was bad, really bad. “All that for me?”

“It was inevitable anyway, I just helped put you in the situation, and you fought for life harder,” Death said.

I was sad for a moment but glad to be alive.

"You were prone to sickness, so I tried to take advantage of that," Death began, "but who survives pneumonia half a dozen times? Each time you fought and fought and never for a moment gave up. It grew almost laughable to see something thrown at you, you almost falling and then popping back up. It is like the miserable dipping bird water toy. It always just keeps going."

"I always liked those things. The one with the red water in its belly was my favorite," I laughed. Death smiled again.

“I grew fond of the game.” He continued, “Everything from the first bomb you made, to the flamethrower. Each time I added a method of us meeting, you overcame it. The ultimate was when the motorcycle crashed into the hole I put there, you remember, the wheel stuck, and you flew over. Who would have thought you would have rolled out of it." Death seemed to smile knowingly. He reached over and touched my head again, and memories flooded me, from the first time I made gunpowder to cannons, to hitting shotgun shells with a hammer. The beatings from kids that were long since gone. Guns pointed at me, but nothing happening, cuts, bruises, and more, but nothing fatal. All this and more flooded into me.

"I understand," I said, "but I am still not sure why I am here."

"Well," Death said, "as we continued our dance there was a day your plane flipped upside down, and you smiled and comforted the other passengers even though it was your first time in a plane. I realized on that day that perhaps I was approaching it the wrong way."

"How so?" I asked, interested.

"There will come a time soon that you will have to leave this world," Death said.

"Soon," I asked.

"Remember for me this is less than an instant, so cut me some slack," Death said, and I smiled. "Obviously, I am not here to take you. I have not set anything up, just our meeting."

I looked at him seriously for a minute, "When Andrew..."

Death actually looked down, "Yes, I set that up. I was hoping to push you to a limit. When he was hit, he too should have died, but he fought. Remember, you have 3 children that should not be either because you should not be. I tried to take him, but as you held his hand in the ER, he felt your warmth, and when he said he was cold and you begged to take anything from you, I spared his life and took your dog instead."

I began crying for a moment, then dried my tears, "She loved him too, I wish she understood."

"She did Andrew," Death said and reached over in a surprisingly compassionate move, "Someday you will know how dogs see humans, and it is beyond your imagination."

I looked up, "You were saying before?"

"Yes, my purpose for today," Death started again, "When I finally come for you, I have seen something in you I have enjoyed. I will allow your line to continue, but you will need to do something for me." He paused for a second, "I occasionally like to take time off, and I will allow you to stand in for me for a while, all you have to do is agree."

"For how long?" I asked.

"Does it matter? A few years or a few hundred thousand are the same, you will not know, and you will learn and love in a new way, perhaps more to your liking?" Death said. "You do not have to answer today, but when I come, I will need an answer."

I smiled, "So there is a possibility of forever."

"There is always forever, no matter what. You will have even more." Death smiled.

"So why tell me?" I asked.

"Imagine at the end having to face all I just showed you and told you, it would be too much. I need you to at least consider this. In a few moments you will wake up, and think this is a dream, and that is ok. You have to know inside, though, I have opened your mind to more possibilities." Death said.

"I get it," I said, "but one thing." Death smiled at my statement. "I can use a sword rather than the sickle?" I asked.

Death laughed, “You truly do make me smile. Who would have thought.”

I heard the door lock behind me and glanced at the girl closing the Coffeetree. “I guess we need to get our drinks to go,” I said.

We laughed for a moment, and the room began to grow darker.

“Smile Andrew, every day is a challenge for you to overcome, and I will always be out here, somewhere, watching over you.” Death whispered.

I woke with a start. I looked at the window and it was dark now. My nap had only been a few minutes, but I had seen a lot. I considered what I had seen and decided to record it. After all, I needed to consider it all for a time someday in the future. I had a lot to think about, but who can really turn down Death? Someday, perhaps I would know. For today I looked out the window and smiled at a Universe full of possibilities.

Down the Drain

"I know I should not have cheated, but what is he going to do?" she thought as she threw her keys on the table. After all, he was not giving her what she needed. The house was dark, yet dim lights jumped in the distance.

"I left the shower running," she heard her wimp of a husband yell, "I knew you would need it."

He had caught her just a few hours before with the stupid hotel bellman at the hotel she worked at. At first, he had first been forceful, but as she told him he would have to get out, he had begged her for another chance and left crying.

"Imagine, crying," she said to herself. "This will be a fun night."

She thought she smelled gasoline, but it went away as she walked down the candlelit hallway into the bedroom. She stripped her clothes confidently, still feeling the slight stickiness from her earlier encounter and anticipating the feel of their fantastic shower.

"At least he is good for something," she thought as she considered the four shower heads that he had installed in their plush shower. The pressure was set so finely it almost stung when she took showers, but she liked it, she liked it a lot.

The candlelight continued, and she considered turning the lights on but knew this was some wimp way of getting her to stay with him. She wondered when he would show up. She heard the shower running, the tinkle of water hitting the glass and tile.

Smiling, she stepped into the steamy shower and the needle-like pinpricks hit her at once, he had done a good job, and no matter where you stood, there was always water hitting you. As she closed the shower door, she saw a shadow, heard a click, and then the sound of a drill.

"What are you doing wimp?" she yelled with a defiant tone.

She heard his voice, sullen, calm, powerful and direct. "Cleaning up my life."

A moment later she heard a gas engine start. It sputtered to life, gasping at air then grabbed hold with mechanical fury. That is when the pain began. The needle-like pinches from the shower became growling bites as they were propelled into her skin. She screamed and turned to the door and pushed. She beat at the door and pressed her body on the glass. The door would not give, as she turned around the skin from her back was cut away by the high-pressure stream of water. She screamed again. "Let me out" she cried as she tried to block the jets only to feel the water rip into her more quickly.

"I am letting you out," he said quietly, "You said our marriage was down the drain, but I think it will just be you going down the drain."

Her skin flayed from her body as she slapped the door with her now blood covered hand. She felt light-headed and as she turned, saw part of her arm fall to the tile with the ever-increasing pieces of flesh ripped from her body by the high-pressure jets. As she passed out, she asked herself if it was worth it, but the answer never came as she slumped to the floor, jets slowly reducing her flesh and even her bones to liquid, to be washed down the shower drain, gone forever.

Outside the door, her husband slumped against the sink and said simply, "Another marriage down the drain." Then he got up and left the room as the shower continued to do its work.

For the Taking

Her grey hair twisted in the light breeze.

Her golden eyes still shimmered yet the lines in her face were almost painful in their bite. She sighed as she walked through the starlit park. It had been so long. As it approached midnight she walked to the shore and watched the stars, it was funny, she remembered far more stars in the sky then glanced around at the city lights and realized that they stole the light from the stars, or at least made them less visible.

She watched diligently and smiled as a shooting star crossed in front of her, a sign of luck, but was it luck she had, or luck to come.

"Hi," she heard a deep voice say behind her.

She turned, looked at the young man. He was in his late 20s, dressed in jeans and a t-shirt with some non-descript heavy metal band plastered on the front of it.

"You got any money?" he said.

"No," she said back to him quietly, eyes darting in several directions looking for any help that could be found.

"Yeah," he said, "I bet you do." he said powerfully. "I think you got some money."

"Please," she said, "please no."

His eyes looked over her grey outfit and focused on the dangling silver choker, the grey gem hung beneath it swaying between her slightly wrinkled breasts. Her grey top looked old and tattered and the white flower in her hair seemed to be long dead, or silk. He was almost appalled at the woman before him, but she still had a nice figure. He might get out of here with two wins.

Stepping forward, he grabbed her grey hair and pulled her to him. His breath was stale and sour as he looked down at the silver amulet, noting the cross and heart and smiling to himself. He felt her body against his and held her hair tight as he worked his arm between them, first reaching for the choker and template, but instead grabbing her breast roughly.

She looked panicked as she rapidly glanced from side to side and he growled at her, "No baby, no help coming."

He pulled her face forward and kissed her roughly as he continued groping her almost violently, then he felt the sting as she bit his lip.

He pulled back and touched the blood on his lip as he held her hair and looking up at her frantic face, he saw a streak of darker hair around the light pink flower in her hair.

She looked side to side again as he said, "You shouldn't have done that". Then he slapped her across the face harshly. Forcefully, he pulled her close again and kissed her roughly tasting his blood as he smeared it on her lips.

She closed her eyes and worked her arms around him, then kissed him back. Her tongue found his mouth and worked around his lips, reveling in the sweet salty taste of his blood. He felt flushed as her tongue worked its way into his mouth and found his willing. She worked it hard, and he felt as though this woman knew his needs better than he did. As their tongues fought a passionate battle her hands found him, and he gasped slightly as electricity seemed to flow between them. He felt her pert breasts push into him as her tongue continued its relentless push in his mouth and somehow, he felt as though he was losing control.

She opened her eyes for only a moment to look from side to side once more, they were still alone. She felt his hardness and it made her even more fervent in her goals as her tongue plunged into his throat. She felt him squirm as the flush came over her, he was trying to pull away, but only a little as she felt him spasm in her hand, and as she kissed him deeply, he seemed to whimper, then cry, then her orgasm came, almost surprising her as she convulsed with spasms against him.

She pulled away and stepped back as he stood uneasily. His grey hair shimmered in the starlight, the light from his eyes was gone and he looked down at his gnarled hands and felt the pain grasping at him. As he looked up at her he saw the brilliant red flower in her flowing red hair. Her skin was brilliant alabaster, and her lips like rose petals as she smiled at him. Her necklace no longer silver, but ruby, and silver, and more ruby sparkling in the starlight with a life of its own. Her perfect body was evident in the black camisole, and she smiled briefly, then simply said, "thank you."

He fell to his knees, crying, looking at his hands, lost in some Alzheimer's induced nightmare that only he could see, and as she walked away in the darkness of the night, she was happy, yet a tear escaped her eyes as once again she had taken, and someday, she would have to again.

Protect His Heart

He was just not that lucky. She was just too perfect and presented herself in such a way that he couldn't resist. Her flowing highlighted hair drifted over her face and those blue eyes peeked out from time to time, beckoning to him, calling to him. As he sat in the bar fiddling nervously with his drink, he considered why he was there. Another failed relationship, another night alone, and the small wine bar offered a place he could unwind, but this woman kept looking over, and he could barely contain himself considering she might just be looking at him.

He decided there was no way it could be true, and he looked away, and as he sat looking at the window, he heard the seat next to him creak. He turned, and she was there.

"Hi," she said quietly.

He stammered, not sure what to say, he felt his face flush and was concerned, even more than he had ever been with the few miserable relationships he had been in. He stressed as he thought about all the women who had hurt him, how bad it felt, how horrible it was to experience the pain and the loss. He shuddered as he looked side to side and his thoughts were broken by the words she spoke, "The answer you should give is "hi"" she said in a wonderfully melodic voice.

"Umm, hi," he said.

She smiled at him, her teeth glinting white in the light of the small wine bar, he saw a glint of metal, but she sipped a drink of her wine, and it was gone.

"You look lonely," she said. "I am not being forward; I just know how it is to be lonely. Everyone I am ever with treats me so poorly and I always seem to end up hurt."

He calmed slightly, "Yeah, I know what you mean."

She continued, "I mean, why can't I just find someone special, someone who will protect my heart, like I want to protect theirs?"

"I know," he said, "People can be so mean, and I never seem to find anyone who wants to be nice, they want to beat up my heart and rend it, and not treat it right at all." He did not know this woman, but he opened up and wondered why he was doing so.

"It is just so complicated," she said. "Anyway, I just wanted to say hi because you looked so lonely."

"Thanks," he said while noticing her again. She wore a simple outfit that she made look stunning. Her near perfect figure was accentuated by a beautiful face, and stunning eyes that seemed to peer through his soul.

"Hi sweetie," she said looking into his eyes as he stared.

He turned away noticing her smile, and she leaned forward and kissed him on the cheek, "Don't worry," she said, "You will find someone to protect your heart." She smiled and laid a $20 on the bar and nodded at the bartender and began to leave. "Bye sweetie," she said with a smile and walked out the door almost silently.

As he was saying bye he noticed the door closed and was sad to be alone once more.

He drank his wine in peace and about 10 minutes later, paid his bill and headed out to his car.

His black Mustang waited for him at the back of the lot, and as he walked there, he noticed a white SUV cranking its engine. He kept walking to his car and started to get in when he saw the woman get out of the SUV and lift the engine compartment.

He stopped, considered, and walked to the SUV. "Problems?" he asked.

"Dumb car," she said, "It was never well taken care of and I try so hard, but it is not working right again."

"Want me to look?" he asked her quietly, not knowing really what to do but willing to try to help this exotic lady.

"Actually, could you help me out and run me home?" she asked. "I will have it towed in the morning."

"Umm, sure," he said. "I would be happy to."

She closed the hood on the SUV and pulled her keys and a purse out of the car, then walked to him and they walked over to his Mustang. The car was new, and still shined as though it had been taken from the lot yesterday. The black finish of the car seemed to absorb the light while reflecting it making it wonder if it had a soul or was stealing one. He opened her door and let her in the passenger side, then got in himself.

The throaty roar of the car rumbled as he started it and he asked her, "Where to?"

She gave him an address that he put in the navigation, then he began driving the few minutes it would take to get there. They talked on the way, about everything and nothing, her job, his job, her life, his lack of a life, her family, his lack of a family and so it went. As they pulled into a more affluent neighborhood the homes got larger and larger, and soon the GPS spoke he had arrived. The house was massive, a front half-moon drive with a 4-car garage to the side, a huge yard, pool, sitting area, high deck and a stunning view.

He gasped, "This is yours?"

"Yes," she said, "A gift from my ex-husband. He did not want it and it was my dream."

"Nice dream," he said.

"Want to come in?" she asked.

"Umm," he said, "I am not sure I should."

She smiled, "Sure you can, come in for one last drink, I will show you around."

He smiled nervously wondering how this woman could have any interest in him and said, "OK."

She walked in front of him to the door and opened it while he was mesmerized by the sway of her body, the look of her. They walked into the house, and he looked at the staircase reaching up to the second floor in front of him. The house was decorated straight out of Restoration Hardware or Pottery Barn and was perfectly clean. Everything looked to be in its place, with books stacked perfectly on tables, begging to be read, and pictures on the wall of long-lost locations that only the photographer knew.

She turned to him, walked back and put her arms around his neck, his heart was beating so fast now as she leaned in and kissed him. He almost felt faint from the feeling.

"Don't worry," she said, "I will protect your heart."

He leaned forward and kissed her and felt like the world was melting around him, he was suddenly so excited he could barely contain himself.

She slowly pulled back, and he followed her almost comically trying to hold the kiss. "In here," she said, and lead him down the hall to the right into a huge bedroom. The bed was a California king, and the room was sparsely decorated except for a dresser and a large curio with colored music boxes in it. He recognized the boxes because he had given one to his ex-girlfriend years ago with a stuffed animal in it.

"Nice collection," he said looking at the boxes as she smiled and began kissing him again. She began undressing him and undressing herself, slowly kicking off her clothes as he did as well. There was a door behind her, and she leaned on it and it opened into a huge bathroom. She walked into the room, her naked hips swaying as she held his hand and he followed obediently to the massive shower.

He felt as though he was going to explode as she bent in front of him and straightened a bathmat, she picked up a towel and dropped it into an overly large laundry chute to the side then stepped into the shower and turned on the water. Then she reached to the counter, and he saw a music box like the others, just an ornate dark blue box, she opened, and it began to play the song "Hero".

The room quickly started to get steamy, and he was confused a little, but she beckoned him, "Hi sweetie." she said with those glinting eyes, and he stepped into the shower. She was as tall as he and they lined up perfectly as she kissed him, he was so excited he felt as though his heart would explode. He stopped for a moment, and she looked him in the eye and said, "Don't worry, I will protect your heart."

He smiled, unsure, and she took soap from a dispenser and rubbed it on his arms, his chest, he felt her against him, the swirl of emotions was replaced by passion, by lust. She rubbed his chest, and the soap was so smooth, so clean. He closed his eyes as she rubbed his chest, and he barely felt the knife cut through his sternum. He gasped for a moment, but the knife had cut deep and as he struggled meekly in surprise he looked into her eyes, the last words he heard were "I will protect your heart" as he saw his heart wrenched from his chest, the panic within him welled up and was gone, then all went dark.

She stood in the shower, the water running over her body and washing the blood down the drain. She held his heart carefully as she washed it in the water ever so gently. The huge shower left a lot of room and the multiple jets of hot water kept washing the blood down the drain until the heart was completely clean. Her body clean as well, she stepped out and wrapped herself in a towel, then took a second towel and dried his heart ever so carefully. "Hero" played on the music box to her side, and she smiled as she looked at the heart and gently placed it in the music box, then closed the lid and felt empty as the music stopped.

Naked, she walked into the bedroom, opened the cabinet, and put the music box on a shelf next to the dozens of others.

Walking back into the bathroom, she went into the shower and lifted his naked body easily, then took his lifeless corpse to the laundry chute. She looked down at his face, and lightly kissed his lips, then pushed his body into the chute.

She knew the chute led to a massive septic digester deep under the house, and over time he would be no more, gone from the world like a silent wisp.

She dressed, got in his car, and went to the still open bar. Wiping the car down, she left it where it was parked before, went to her car, and, flipping a small switch, turned the key and it started instantly. As she plugged in her phone a graphic popped on the screen, a simple red heart with the words "Protect his heart" came on and she smiled knowing that is exactly what she did, and exactly what she would do.

The Edge

The secondhand store was unique. The walls and shelves were covered with items ranging from the sublime to the ridiculous. There was no rhyme or reason to any of it, it looked as though someone had strewn items in a room and just needed them to fit like an immense Jenga game.

On one shelf a Barbie playhouse tightly packed next to a carburetor for an unknown car. On another shelf an unstrung crossbow lay while being covered with mid-70s vinyl albums. It was a parade of plethora, a cavalcade of stuff.

"What are we doing here?" Karen Klay asked her friend.

"We are looking for something to put on my empty wall," Alexandra answered. Alexandra Xavier Cross was a young woman of 25. She was thin and had long brown hair flowing well past her shoulders. Alexandra walked with a cane and had a limp from an older accident. The accident had left her struggling to walk, and she hated every moment of it.

"You don't have an empty wall," Karen laughed. Karen's short red hair made her look more like a pixie than a person. She was petite and overly animated at all times.

"Sure, I do, between the bathroom and the bedroom," Alexandra laughed.

"Oh, that six-inch spot that looks like a strip of white? I get it."

"It is bigger that six inches. I just like to use the space. You know that," Alexandra smiled. "So what if I like my room more decorative than your four bare walls."

"Touché," Karen laughed. "How about this?" Karen said as she picked up a long wrench with a bolt attached all neatly mounted on a wood frame."

"I am not a mechanic," Alexandra laughed. "But that is pretty cool, right?"

The two rummaged through the piles of items left by forgotten owners who either threw them away or sold them to the small store. As they went through each item, they both found nice uses or laughs about it. The kitchen items were the hit of the trip as they both admitted they did not cook well and lived on fast food and cheap microwave items.

After about 30 minutes of looking Alexandra found a long narrow wooden box. The box was incredibly ornate. The wood seemed incredibly strong and though obviously very old, it held no scar or scratch. On the front were a series of small sliding blocks that seemed to move freely, each was decorated with a Roman Numeral, and each numeral could freely flow from side to side. Setting her cane down Alexandra pulled the box out completely. It stood almost 4 feet tall, and someone had added a mounting point to the back. As she looked at the mount, she saw scratches where someone tried to nail or screw in the mount, then glued it to the back. Whatever the wood was it was very durable.

"Whatcha got?" Karen asked.

"Not sure," Alexandra replied. "But it looks nice."

"What's it say?" Karen pointed to some writing below the designs.

Alexandra strained to see and finally the ornate cursive seemed to come into focus, "Et potestas vitam et mortem" Alexandra replied. Which doesn’t make a lot of sense, it means kinda the power of life and death."

"You should get it, it sounds just like you," Karen giggled. "It would fit on your wall as well. We need to go anyway; Greg is coming over tonight and you know how he gets."

Alexandra steadied herself with her cane and picked up the rather heavy wooden piece. As she did she saw that the whole box was ornate, but it looked as though it could have a crease in it. It really didn't matter. She would clean it up later. Karen saw her struggle and started to get the box, but Alexandra frowned at her, "I got it."

The two worked their way to a makeshift counter covered in papers and assorted flotsam.

"I see you found the box," the gruff man with a 10-day shadow and greasy hair said.

"Yeah," Karen said, "We sure found a box. How much?"

"Ha," The man laughed, showing his yellowing smile. "The man who sold that to me said it is the ultimate source of power and would be the most amazing find ever."

"Why would he give it up then?" Karen asked.

"Well, my price to him was right of course," The man had to be at least 70, and the smell was obvious.

"I can see you stock such fine artifacts," Karen laughed.

The man smirked, "I think we can come to a fair price easily."

"Why did the man sell it?" Alexandra asked in a direct tone.

"I am not sure," The man said, "but my price was fair."

"I think you know," Alexandra was stern.

The man eyed her, "According to the man this was supposed to be the find of the century, but it was just a box, and he needed cash."

"So not that source of ultimate power," Alexandra said.

"Well, not as far as he knew, he said he could not find how it worked." The man replied.

"How much?" Alexandra pushed.

"It is priceless," the man replied.

"Then with no price I should leave it," Alexandra stated and set the box down and began to move away.

"Wait wait," the man spasmed, "You are shrewd, aren't you? Make me an offer."

"An offer for this priceless artifact, I would surely hurt your feelings. I am a poor cripple with little money." Alexandra eyed him as she spoke.

"Make an offer," the man added immediately.

"How about twenty dollars." Alexandra said as she distanced herself from the box.

The old man eyed her and touched the box, "Look at this craftmanship, surely you know it should be at least a hundred dollars, not twenty. The wood itself is worth more than that."

"I am poor, I can't afford any more," Alexandra lowered her head slightly, "Let's go Karen." Alexandra began walking towards the door.

"Wait, wait, wait," The man said, "I see how you are, a hard case. You want a real deal, fifty dollars cash out the door." Alexandra kept walking. "Twenty-five dollars."

Alexandra spun on her cane and said, "Done."

"I think I have been taken," the old man said as Alexandra held out her hand with a twenty and a five in it.

"You would have rather taken me," Alexandra said. "Where did it come from?"

"I wasn't lying about that part. The man who gave it to me said it was the ultimate source of power, but he didn't know how to use it."

"He gave it to you?" Karen said.

"He got what he wanted. It has been here for a while, gathering dust." The man laughed. The smell was obnoxious from his breath.

Alexandra took the long box again and began walking out, as she got to the door she said, "I'll let you know if I become all powerful." She and Karen walked out into the night.

Their loft was only a short walk away. The upper floor of a warehouse had been converted into an apartment while the warehouse remained below. It was all Alexandra had in the world, and it gave her an OK living after taxes, and all the repairs. Her father had left her the building and it was close enough to school she had no issue getting there, and close enough to downtown that they could walk for everything. The walks did her good and kept her legs from degrading further.

The building was dark, but the lights burned all around as they approached. Motion sensing LEDs did their job and the two were bathed in a frosty glow. They chatted about everything, and Alexandra was struggling with the box, but Karen knew better than to ask twice to help. Alexandra's temper was a legend in her college for her outburst if she felt someone was catering to her. She was not one to give up. The doctors had told her the damage would degrade until she could no longer walk in 3 months. That was years ago, she struggled but did not fall.

Karen opened the big steel door, and they walked in, closed the door, and clicked on the concrete until they reached the elevator. It was a huge freight elevator, probably more powerful than most bulldozers as it could carry auto parts up and down floors with no strain. Karen turned the key that allowed it to move, and they took it to the top floor and walked out into their loft.

"Greg should be here soon, you need anything?" Karen asked.

"Dump him?" Alexandra chided.

"You always say that," Karen laughed, "He is not so bad."

"You always say that, he and his friends give me the creeps," Alexandra said. "They are always eyeing everything like we have money or something. Worse, he treats you like a sex object."

"Maybe I like being treated like a sex object," Karen said, "After all, you were always the 'exotic beauty' and I was the tag-a-long friend."

"Whatever," Alexandra said and walked to her room while Karen walked the other way smiling. As she reached the door she turned, "You know I wouldn't care if I did not love you like my sister. I just don't want you to get hurt."

Karen turned, they stared for a minute, "Yeah, I know." Karen said, "I love you too." They both looked, Karen wiped a tear, then she turned and walked to her room.

Their rooms were separated, and the floor fairly finished. It was once offices and now worked well as a large apartment. They could have had 10 people stay as most of the rooms were empty. Alexandra lived in a modest way, she wanted the money to last.

Beneath her, the parts factory raged during the day, but at night it was quiet. In truth, during the day it was just the light drone of machinery and was not an issue.

In her room, she put her newfound treasure on the king-sized bed. The walls of the room were covered with everything. It would have been as bad as the store she was just at except there was some sort of makeshift pattern to it all. The knick-knacks were pretty, clean, and well arranged. Alexandra went to the small wall space that was empty and looked at it. She thought it would work well. Walking back to the bed she examined the box and noted the symbols again. A drawer next to her bed offered several cleaning supplies. Seated on her bed, she began cleaning the box and studying the numbers.

It was not long before the box looked almost new. The smudges of some epoxy on the back were not noticeable from the front, so it was all good. She played with the numbers. They moved a little from side to side, so she started cleaning around them. Soon they slid more freely. A little bit of Endust and it was even more freely.

The numbers were all Roman numerals and by moving them around she could bring only 4 to the top. There were four Is, four Vs and four Xs, followed by 4 Cs. Only 4 could fit on top. She arranged the numbers to be IIII, to no change. She did the same with each and there was no change.

"Why am I doing this?" she asked herself out loud. A silly block of wood with a Chinese puzzle on it means nothing. Alexandra got off her bed with a little difficulty, swung her leg around and pulled a wall hanger and a hammer out of the drawer. She walked to her wall, measured and hammered the hanger in. With effort she put away the hammer and grabbed the box. Using it to counterweight herself she walked to the wall and placed the box in the middle. It was a perfect fit. Two inches on either side.

The numbers had slid from the top spot. She moved them around so they would not slide down and slid four number up. VIXI. The box clicked. A seam appeared where she had not even noticed one.

"Oh crap," Alexandra said to herself.

She left the box on the wall and with minimal force pulled at the front, it slid open with ease on some type of dowel hinges. The light glinted off sparkling steel. A sword was inside of the box. It had a single blade about 3 feet long, with a red hilt adding another 5 inches. It was clean, looking like it had just been purchased or made with no imperfections. The cross guard was not normal. The quillons were not just ornate, they were both blades that gave the bearer the ability to use them offensively as well. On the hilt the numbers were there VIXI.

Alexandra grabbed her phone from her purse on the bed and moved back to the displayed sword. She looked up VIXI and a few restaurants came up, but there it was, VIXI number. It might mean "I have lived" or "My Life is over" or "I'm dead". It made no sense.

She was timid but curious and she moved her hand closer and closer until she touched the hilt. She jerked back right away, there was nothing there. She laughed a little, nervous, and touched it again for a moment longer. Nothing happened. There were two slots around the hilt and one smaller, one larger. She put her thumb in the smaller and her fingers in the larger and felt the hilt in her closed fingers. She braced the box but did not need to as the sword came free in her hand easily.

There was no weight to it. It felt as though she were holding paper. She touched the metal, and it was neither warm nor cold. It did not even feel like it was there except her finger stopped as she touched the side. The edges looked sharp, and she did not want to test that on her finger like the idiots in import stores who cut themselves often. She walked to her dresser, opened the second drawer and pulled out a washcloth she used for cleaning.

"Fingerprints first," Alexandra said out loud. She wiped the fingerprints off the blade, and as she did the cloth rolled over the edge, and the piece fell to the ground, cut in a perfect straight line where it has fallen.

"Oh wow," Alexandra said as she gingerly placed the sword on the bed. It lay there on her black bedspread, gleaming in the LED light.

The music began blaring behind her. It was near deafening. Screamo rock started assailing her ears. It was not that she did not like it, she just was not in the mood for it. Alexandra liked all music there were times for anything that was musical, this was just not the time. She walked out of her room into the center area that server as the living room and there was Karen and 3 men, Greg in the middle of them. Greg was handsome and six-foot, dark hair, and green eyes. He would have looked more handsome if his face was not covered with tattoos. Alexandra did not care about tattoos, she had several herself, but his face was marred by them.

The second man was big, probably near 7 feet. He had massive arms and looked like a man mountain. His head was close-shaven and gleamed in the light. The big man's name was Moose, or at least that is what they called him. The third man reminded Alexandra of a squirrel, or a rat, or something similar. His face was pointy and misshapen, his teeth distended, and his eyes darted everywhere, right now, everywhere on Alexandra. They had always called him Skiff, and it fit.

"Can you guys turn it down?" Alexandra said.

Karen giggled then laughed, then her head fell back while she was in Greg's arms. Alex felt nervous and sick. She hobbled to Karen.

"What's wrong with her?" Alexandra asked.

"She's taking a trip," Greg laughed and Alexandra saw the needle marks.

"She would never," Alexandra said, "She doesn't do drugs."

The squirrel like man laughed, "She does now!" He giggled like a man insane and chortled almost simultaneously making him even more grotesque.

Alexandra reached her and tried to open her eyes, but they were rolled back in her head. She was barely breathing, her face light blue as though she were suffocating.

"She needs a doctor!" Alexandra said frantically.

"She is fine," Greg laughed, "Can you believe she tried to dump me tonight. Nobody dumps me."

"Yeah, nobody." the big man said.

"She needs a doctor," Alexandra said and turned and walked towards her room.

"No, no, no," The big man said as he grabbed Alexandra's hair and lifter her off the ground. "No cops or nothin."

Greg laughed and watched Alexandra's feet dangle. She jerked from side to side while holding his hand to keep from pulling her hair. Kicking hard she hit him a few times. The big man held her up and slapped her as he dropped her.

Alexandra fell with a thud and sprawled out on the floor. She hurt all over, and her leg felt horrible. She scuffled on her side towards her room. If she could only get to her phone. She had to save Karen. She looked at her and felt the blood from her lip hit her arm.

The three men were laughing, and Karen was like a ragdoll in Greg's arms. Alexandra looked to her door, it was there, feet away, she pushed harder angry at her inability to move. Her anger gave her strength, and nothing would stop her. She felt the boot hit her legs and knock her down again. Alexandra pulled herself up on her arms and worked her way towards the bedroom, she had reached the door when she was kicked again. The pain wrenched her, and the wind was knocked out of her. Her dresser was beyond the door, her purse and phone only inches away. She pulled herself up on the dresser nearly fainting from the pain. As she reached for her phone Skiff sent her flying to the bottom of the bed with another brutal kick.

He looked at the dresser and saw her phone. "Oh, did you want this?" His eyes were filled with insanity. He looked out the door and said, "Greg, I gots her phone. She is mine now. You guys can have seconds." He laughed and giggled and shut the door.

Alexandra pulled herself up and leaned against the bed. Karen did not have much time left, Skiff turned towards her. "I always thought you looked good." He walked to her and hit her across the face. The pain was horrible. She wanted to cry, but she wouldn't, nothing was going to make her cry. He spun her around and ripped her shirt up the back touching her skin. His vile touch made her skin crawl. She screamed as he threw her forward face down on the bed and began ripping at her pants.

"Noooo!" Alexandra screamed.

"Oh yeah," Skiff said, "You are going to like this, you know you will."

She reached back for him, and he pushed her arms forward with his.

Her clothes were giving out, she opened her fingers, and felt warmth in her hand. Her eyes were blurred but she saw the red hilt in her hand. It felt warm, not like it should, but warm, inviting, it was amazing. She kicked back as Skiff tried yet another angle to remove her pants and it caught him and she swung.

The blade felt like air. No, it felt like a jump rope swinging in her hand. It was not real that this long sword was as light as air. Skiff saw her swing and did not see anything coming. The blade entered his chest between the 4th and fifth rib. It did not slow, nor did Alexandra feel the blade catch, it went through, through his sternum, and out the other side. She felt as though she would lose her balance, but the blade held no weight. Skiff looked at her with an odd expression as his body fell in half.

Alexandra gasped, not because of what happened but because as his body began to fall it shimmered and turned to ash, then dust, then nothing. The hilt felt warm, and Alexandra looked down and the blade glowed. Alexandra jerked for a minute and pushed the blade down to steady herself, it embedded into the floor as she held herself and caught her breath.

She felt better, her face and the pain she was feeling was nearly gone, a slight memory. Alexandra touched her face, and the cut on her lip was gone. The hilt was still warm, but she felt very different. The biggest difference was her leg did not hurt. It had hurt for so long she always ignored it, but now in this moment, there was no pain.

"Karen," she said, "Karen!" she screamed. Alexandra pulled the sword from the floor easily noticing it had sunk nearly an inch beyond the wood floor. She was sure the concrete below had stopped it.

Moose walked in the door, "Where's Skiff?"

"He had to get cleaned up." Alexandra said as she walked towards Moose. She was scared but thrilled, she was walking, and it did not hurt. She was walking and she felt good.

"Where is Skiff?" Moose yelled as he dove for her.

Alexandra's move was clumsy, but she brought the sword up then down straight. The blade entered Moose at the top of his head, and as before it kept going with no drag nor stop until it passed through his genital's. The hilt felt warm again, and a moment later Moose fell, in two pieces and two different directions. Alexandra was amazed at how much detail she could see, the veins and arteries were there, but they looked frozen in time, she could see the stomach and even some of what he must have eaten, intestines, liver, and even a bit of the heart, but as before when Moose began to fall he shimmered to ash, then dust, and then not even a trace remained.

As Moose disappeared Greg came into focus. Alexandra felt odd, powerful, strong, perhaps even more than strong. The hilt felt very warm if not hot in her hand, and she saw the blade of the sword had begun to glow a light blue.

"What the..." Greg said as Alexandra walked towards him.

"Karen needs a doctor," Alexandra yelled.

"Karen needs nothing," Greg said as he reached behind himself and pulled out a gun. "What did you do to Moose?" Greg screamed, "Where is Skiff?" He boomed again.

Karen looked bad, she had vomit on her face, she looked light blue and Alexandra was sure she would die soon.

Greg brandished the weapon again, "Where are they?" he squealed like an insane pig.

"I just want Karen," Alexandra said. "I don't want her to die."

A tear fell, Alexandra couldn't remember the last time she cried about anyone or anything. She was worried. She didn't know what to do, Karen was dying or dead.

The shots rang out and Alexandra saw the flash of light. She thought she did at least, she heard 6 shots and saw the flash each time. It was fast, so fast, but she thought she saw the bullets coming towards her. They looked comical as though they were from a cartoon gun, and she moved out of the way then watched the bullets pass her. It was an odd sensation and her heart felt calm, and she felt at ease. She was at the side of Greg, and he turned at her, looked at her and gasped.

"What the..." he began as he dropped Karen's lifeless body. She hit with a crunch but gasped a little. She was still alive. Alexandra looked at the man next to her holding the gun in disbelief and knew what she had to do. She plunged the blade into his chest, and it entered with no resistance, then she swung outwards, and the blade came free while the gun clattered to the floor. As it did, she knelt and grabbed Karen's hand and held it on the hilt with hers. She covered their hands together.

As Greg began to fall there was a look of astonishment in his eyes, he turned to ash, then dust, then nothing and Alexandra felt the now familiar warmth. She looked at Karen, her face pink once more, her breathing more regular. Still, she was asleep. Alexandra set the sword down and started to drag her to her room. She moved easily. Far too easily. Taking a chance, Alexandra tried and successfully picked her up. She was in shock with her newfound strength. She carried Karen to her room, lay her on the bed, and covered her with her blanket.

Walking back to the living area she turned off the music and picked up the sword. There was no scratch nor blemish, nor imperfection anywhere. It was warm and felt good in her hands.

Alexandra spun the blade in her hand, and went to her room, she walked with no limp to the wall where the box hung, case open and as she had removed it she placed it in the case. "From death, life." Alexandra smiled. She closed the box and wondered about the origin of the blade. She had found it, or maybe it had found her, and what would come next would be an adventure.

Faith

Agatha Fairchild was annoyed at the repeated knocking at her door. Agatha had very few visitors and wanted far fewer. Agatha surveyed her plush furnishings scattered throughout the spacious living room as she glided through towards the foyer. She noted with some annoyance that there was dust on some of the curios and made a note to herself that she would clean and polish those areas today after she dealt with whatever annoyance was coming her way. Agatha was a tall woman with crisp features that could easily have been mistaken for royalty and even aged 70 years she still radiated beauty. Agatha's silver hair was in a tight bun on top of her head and she checked the bun and tightened it as she reached the foyer and the offending door.

The door rapped again, and Agatha grimaced with the upcoming confrontation. The solid cherry door with the ornate stained-glass windows swung open to reveal the secure black security door with bars and bulletproof glass that kept her quite safe from visitors and other people.

On the other side of the door stood a beautiful young woman in a mask with a young girl standing next to her, masked as well. The woman was thin and the child even thinner but not so much they looked ill. The two looked fit and tidy, almost as if they were ready to be in a fitness magazine advertisement. Both had striking blue eyes and the child was full of the youthful inquisitive look that Agatha used to see in children many years ago. The woman's eyes were frantic and puffy. She had obviously been crying over some unknown issue. Agatha instantly recognized them as her neighbors. The woman was Mary, and the child was Faith. She had only seen them with their masks since this horrible disease, but it was the child who stood out. Her eyes danced with an unknown light, and Agatha remembered that all too well.

"What do you want Mary?" Agatha asked.

“I'm sorry Agatha I know you hate visitors and you never really liked us, but I need your help.”

Agatha raised an eyebrow then said, “You need my help?” The last word rung out and she emphasized it with sarcastic weight.

“Please Agatha I will beg if I have to, but I have just gotten the call and my son is in some trouble. I would like to take Faith, but I don't think I should. Please can you watch her for a short time while I get Franklin and bring him home.”

Agatha had not lowered her eyebrow and simply asked, “You want me to watch a child in my home?”

“Please Agatha you know I just moved here and it's just me and the children I have no one in the world but them. She is not a bother, and she will listen to whatever you say.”

“My home is not suitable for children,” Agatha replied, “I don't think it is a good idea.”

“Please Agatha,” Mary asked again, “I will pay you all I can if you will just watch Faith for a short time, it shouldn't be very long, I'm sorry to be an imposition, but I have no one else to turn to.”

“No, I don't think so,” Agatha said as she began to close the door. As she looked down and the door closed, she saw Faith looking up at her. The innocence and inquisitive nature of her eyes said something that Mary never could have. She held the door for a moment. She stared at the child for a brief instant then looked back at Mary.

“2 hours,” Agatha said, “and make no mistake she will have to wear that mask. I don't need any of this Covid-19 in my home.” Agatha opened the security door.

Mary looked down at her daughter. "You listen to everything Agatha says. Do not take off your mask. Remember, you can only take off the mask if you have to eat, and then only a little."

"I will listen Mommy," Faith reaching and holding her mother's hand for a moment. "It will be fine. I won't take off my mask. Get Franklin and make Franklin safe and I will be waiting."

Mary looked up, tears in her eyes with her mask seemingly damp from her crying, then spoke, "Thank you Agatha you don't know what this means."

"Yes, yes," Agatha said with obvious frustration. "Get your boy and get back here. I would hate to have to leave this ragamuffin on your front porch."

Mary looked at her daughter and smiled, but no one could see beneath the mask, she turned and walked to her waiting car. As Agatha and Faith watched from the security door the Pale Silver Impala drove off, then Agatha turned and closed the ornate cherry door.

The door closed Agatha looked down at the little girl. "How old are you?"

The child considered for a moment. "I am almost seven years old ma'am," Faith replied looking up with those sparkling eyes.

"Well," Agatha said as she walked to the living room, "I do not have a TV in this room, and I suppose you have one of those smart phones to keep you busy." She turned; Faith had followed her diligently. "You can occupy yourself."

"No ma'am," Faith said, "I do not have a smart phone or a phone at all, Mommy says little girls don't need all that until they become older and more responsible. I have a book I can read while mommy is gone."

"Read huh?" Agatha replied, "So you know how to read."

"Yes ma'am," Faith said, "I love books. They show you new worlds and take you away from all the bad stuff."

"Indeed," Agatha said, "You seem much older than 7."

"Thank you, ma'am," Faith replied. "Mommy says reading has given me a good vocabulary."

"I will agree," Agatha replied, "Vocabulary is a big word for seven. What are you reading?"

"I am reading Frost right now, his poetry is very good," Faith said, her mask covering a smile that shone brightly in her eyes. "I hope to finish today."

"Really?" Agatha said obviously surprised at the reading level of a 7-year-old. She strained for a moment trying to remember how much she read when she was 7 and could not recall. She looked at the little girl, standing, waiting for her every word. "This is my living room. The couch to the right or the chair to its left will be where you may sit. If I am not in the room, you may remove the mask, but if you can see me the mask must be on, do you understand?"

"Of course, ma'am," Faith replied as she moved to the big armchair with red paisley fabric, "I will leave the mask on and read."

"Very good," Agatha said, "I noticed I need to clean and will be working, so amuse yourself but do not leave this room unless you have to go to the bathroom. If you do the bathroom is in the center hall. Please wash your hands if you do anything and clean up after yourself."

"Yes, ma'am," Faith replied and literally jumped up into the chair holding her book, *The Poetry of Robert Frost*.

Agatha went to the kitchen and got a towel and some Pledge, she returned to the living room and Faith was paying close attention to the book in her hands as her eyes darted back and forth while she read. Her mask was tight on her face, a cute mask with small yellow butterflies on the print. Agatha went to a curio cabinet, sprayed Pledge on her cloth and began cleaning. She noticed Faith had put the book down and she looked to her, "You should keep reading."

"Ma'am, I was wondering if you wanted help?" Faith asked. "You have so many pretty cabinets. I bet it takes a long time to clean them all."

Agatha looked around the room, yes, it was a big job, but she rarely noticed as she did little else but eat, clean, and read. "Will you do a good job?" Agatha asked. "Yes ma'am," Faith replied, "Mommy taught me, and I will do very good for you."

Agatha considered, "Wait here, I will be a moment." Agatha went into the kitchen and got an additional towel, a small stool, and another can of pledge. She considered for a moment and realized the child could overuse the Pledge, but it would not hurt. She returned and handed the linen cloth, Pledge, and small stool to Faith. "You start on this one over here," she showed the young girl to a cherry hutch with ornate claw work and deep engraved scrollwork.

"Yes, ma'am," Faith said and took the cloth and knelt on the floor. Agatha watched as she unfolded and refolded the cloth into a small square, then sprayed the cloth with pledge. She then began to methodically clean the legs of the curio and Agatha almost smiled. She walked back to the curio she was working on and continued her cleaning. After about 10 minutes Faith walked to her.

"What is it?" Agatha asked.

"Do you have some Q Tips ma'am?" Faith asked.

"In the hall bathroom, there are Q Tips on the top of each bathroom counter," Agatha said, and the little girl nodded and walked down the hall. Agatha continued cleaning for several minutes and noticed the little girl was back. The girl was concentrating hard but Agatha could not tell at what, so she walked to the cabinet and looked as Faith was cleaning the scrollwork with a Q Tip. She was being very meticulous as she sprayed the tip, then worked the Q Tip through the scrollwork, wiped the Q Tip off with the towel and continued again. Agatha watched in fascination as she finished and stood up. It was something she had never seen, and she was surprised at the attention to detail that this almost 7-year-old exuded.

"All done ma'am," Faith said, "Would you like me to start the next one?"

Agatha examined the child's work. She looked at the scrollwork and the crispness of it. She could not remember the last time the edges had been so clean. The entire Curio cabinet now looked nearly new. She smiled a small smile and looked at the 4 cabinets in the room. 1 now shone above the rest, there were two yet to do while she was still working on hers.

"Are you sure you would like to keep working?" Agatha asked.

"Yes, ma'am," Faith said. "I like to help, and they are so pretty."

"Do you like the figurines?" Agatha asked.

Faith looked inside and noted that all of the curio cabinets contained porcelain figurines. The one she was working on contained people, the other scenes, one was all animals, and finally one was assorted items.

"Yes ma'am, they are very pretty. The Snow White figurine is very pretty, but all of them are nice." The figurine was clean and showed the girl singing, her long dark hair flowing. The detail was amazing. The figurine held an apple contemplating it with red ribbon in her hair and a flowing cape locked in an eternal wind."

"You know Snow White?" Agatha asked.

"Yes ma'am," Faith replied. "Her book is one of my favorites."

"You have seen the movie?" Agatha asked.

"Yes ma'am." Faith said, "It was a long long time ago and Mommy says we will again someday, but it has been very busy, and we have had to move many times."

"I tell you what," Agatha said, her tone much softer, "If we finish up in time, we can watch the movie."

Faith's eyes twinkled, "Only if we finish though ma'am. We have to do our work to enjoy our play."

Agatha was near taken aback, "Yes child, we have to do our work to enjoy our play."

Faith moved to the second cabinet and began cleaning. She moved the stool as well and was incredibly detail oriented as she polished each inch of the Curio Cabinet.

Agatha finished hers and began on her second as well. Smiling a little at the feeling of getting this chore done. "Faith," she said, "Why have you had to move so much?"

"Well, Father died. He was a doctor and died during the first part of the pandemic," Faith stated with more maturity than her years presented. "After daddy died mommy lost her job. She tried really hard to get another job and daddy left us money, but it is tied up in something with bad men. I think they call it prorate."

"You mean probate?" Agatha asked.

"Yes ma'am, probate," Faith continued. "It will be OK, but mommy is sad all the time, and Franklin is starting to work at the hospital now to help mommy. Mommy is waiting tables. Sometimes the people who rent the houses to us don't want to rent to mommy, so we have to move."

"But money is coming, right?" Agatha asked.

"Yes ma'am, but they don't know when," Faith said. "People have not been nice to mommy. I try to help, but I am still little."

"Do you like your new house?" Agatha asked. She looked back and Faith was cleaning the scrollwork and edging of the curio with a Q Tip.

"Yes ma'am," Faith said, "But mommy said she doesn't know if we will be able to stay."

"I see," Agatha said.

"How are you doing?" Agatha asked.

"I'm almost done." Faith said, "Can I help you now?"

"I am almost done too," Agatha replied. "What about your Grandma or Grandpa, can they help?"

"No ma'am, they died when Franklin was little." Faith said, "We are all alone."

"I see," Agatha said, "I did not think your mommy was very old, but Franklin is older?"

"Yes," Faith replied, "Franklin is" Faith paused for a moment, "Almost 20 years old. I was a good surprise mommy says. She works so hard for Franklin and I."

"I see," Agatha said again.

Agatha stood, "I am done, are you?"

"Yes ma'am," Faith said.

"That just won't do. Call me Aggie or Aunt Aggie if you like, but ma'am is just not right. We can watch the movie in the sitting room. Are you hungry?"

"Yes ma'am," Faith said, "but I have to wait for mommy to eat."

"Oh child, look at how pretty you made my cabinets," Agatha replied a small grin crossing her face as they surveyed their work, "It is the least I can do to thank you."

Faith smiled at the compliment and picked up her cloth, Pledge, and Q Tips.

As Agatha did the same, she said, "Let's go make a snack." The two walked into the spacious kitchen and Agatha took the items from Faith and put them away. She took the rags and walked into a room behind the kitchen and returned with two aprons.

"What would you like to eat?" Agatha asked.

"I should wait for mommy ma'am," Faith said. "She makes sure I am ok when I eat."

"OK?" Agatha asked. "Are you ill?"

"No ma'am," Faith said, "Mommy just likes for me to eat right so she can cleanup if I make a mess."

Agatha looked back at the cabinets, "you seem like such a clean child, but we will wait for your mother." Agatha paused, "and you can call me Aggie or Aunt Aggie instead of ma'am."

"OK Aunt Aggie," Faith replied as they stood in the ornate kitchen.

"You like Snow White?"

"Yes," Faith replied, "I like Snow White because she is a princess and isn't mean. People who are princesses should be nice to people, but mommy said the people who we got houses from asked us to leave, why do they do that? Mommy says they have to make money, but mommy will pay sometime, mommy always writes checks, but she says you have to have money to write checks."

"That's true honey, you have to have money in the bank. I am sure it will work out soon."

"Mommy says the same, but I really don't want to move again," Faith replied, "Since daddy died, we have moved 3 times."

"That's very sad," Agatha replied, "We will have to see what can be done. Should we watch the movie?"

"Only if you want to Aunt Aggie," Faith replied, "I don't want to be a bother."

"It is no bother dear; it is one of my favorite stories," Agatha said. "Let's go in the den and watch the movie together. It will be our little party."

Agatha thought for a moment about all the people who had visited her, of all of them it was a child who had more manners than any. Even her family showed no care or remorse in visiting and leaving the house in a less than perfect state. They were all gone now, and she did not see them often.

Agatha picked out a DVD, took it to a player and turned on a massive TV.

"Wow, that is a big TV," Faith said.

"I almost never use it," Agatha pondered, "I usually just read."

"Me too," Faith replied.

They both laughed as the movie came on. Faith's eyes got wide as the book opened and she smiled and said "I know this part" as the pages turned. Moments later the animation started. The castle drew close and the evil queen came into view.

As the words "Rags cannot hide her gentle grace" were spoken Agatha looked at the young girl next to her and a tear formed in her eye.

Faith seemed mesmerized by the movie and the wishing well song played out before her eyes. She said not a word but watched with an intensity that was fiery as well as patient.

Agatha watched as the movie played out, as much interested in the little girl as the movie but admiring the fantastic commitment and focus of the child. No interruptions or calls upon her. On the screen before her the dwarfs chased the evil queen in her haggard disguise and as the lightning struck Faith jumped and the vultures circled away slowly.

Still Faith did not say a word. Tears formed as the music played and Snow White lay in her crystal coffin. Still the little girl was silent, each tear that fell was matched by Agatha's own. When the prince kissed Snow White and her eyes fluttered open, Faith gasped in joy and watched until she saw the words, "and they lived happily ever after."

As the movie closed Agatha stood and wiped her eyes with a silk kerchief. She walked to a cabinet and pulled another silk kerchief from a drawer and handed it to Faith.

"Thank you, Aunt Aggie," Faith said, "Thank you for everything. The movie was so good it is the bestest day ever."

"What was your favorite part?" Agatha asked with a near childlike innocence in her words.

"It was all my favorite," Faith said, "but I would like to find the wishing well."

"Really?" Agatha asked, "What would you wish for?"

"I would wish for Daddy to be back and for me to be able to eat, but if I couldn't have that I would wish mommy was happy again and we could live happily ever after."

"Are you hungry dear? We should eat." Agatha said, "I can make you anything."

"Mommy said I shouldn't," Faith said.

"Come here child," Agatha said.

Faith walked to her and stood before her; the mask of red roses covered her face perfectly.

"Let's take that mask off and get you something good to eat," Agatha said.

Agatha reached forward and pulled Faith's mask off even as Faith reached for it. The black mask with red roses came away easily and Agatha gasped for a moment. Behind the mask and under the beautiful blue eyes was a mouth that was misshapen into a large circle. It was not so much a mouth as a maw and Agatha was shocked to see the hundreds of needle-like teeth protruding from the gaping hole. She marveled at how each tooth looked like a tiny hypodermic needle and how they seemed to glisten like new porcelain. They were so small, and the child's eyes looked almost sorrowful as she climbed upon the woman's lap and leaned into her. Agatha was shocked that she felt nothing but a shiver as the child's lips met her neck. Should it have hurt? Why me? What was happening? Why couldn't she move? All these questions were on her mind as Agatha soon embraced a final sleep. Faith held her tender and tight rocking slowly on her lap.

Time passed.

The doorbell rang.

The front door opened; it had begun raining again. Faith's mother stood at the front door alone as rain fell on her.

Mary stepped in tentatively, "Faith, where is your mask?"

"Mommy," Faith said, "I am cleaning up."

Mary looked down at Faith, and followed her into the house, closing the door behind them, "Of course."

Mary followed Faith to the den and huge television showed the menu for Snow White. There on the couch sat Agatha, eyes still open and glazed. Her body was white and lifeless now, drained of life and blood by the child who was now carefully cleaning the room. The wounds on her neck we so small as to not be noticed, and there was no trace of blood anywhere.

"Did she take off the mask?" Mary asked.

"Yes," Faith replied. "It was not as I expected. We will be able to get enough money to move to the next city from her accounts. I have the necessary papers on the counter. She has quite a tidy sum put away and no one will miss her for some time."

"That will be good. Your brother did well today and is headed to the next city on our list. I expect we will be able to live in solitude for many years now." Mary said then considered. "What was not as expected?"

"She tried to be nice. I thought we had misread her, and we may have done exactly that. She was just a lonely woman who had no friends or family left, that's all. When she reached for the mask, I did not move away fast enough. I would likely not have hurt her otherwise." Faith said. "She was a nice old lady, but I am full now and no one will miss her." Faith finished cleaning up and looked over the room. She left the TV on and, using the remote, set the movie to play over and over again. "Do you remember when we saw this the day it came out? It was so wonderful back then."

"Yes, it was, it gave so many people hope," Mary said with a slight laugh.

"Yes, it did," Faith replied as they walked to the door, picking up the bank papers as they passed through the kitchen. Faith replaced her black mask with red roses and looked up. "People should have hope, don't you think?"

"Yes," Mary replied as they opened the cherry door and stepped into the rain, "but if they can't have hope, then they should have Faith."

Faith smiled under her mask at the play on words as the two disappeared into the night.

About the Author

Andrew Allen Smith was born in Anderson, Indiana. Until the age of fifteen, he moved at least once per year and finally settled in Lexington, Kentucky. Andrew spent a significant amount of his teenage years reading and writing short stories, attempts at novels, and poetry. He published his first book, "A Slice of Passion," in 2005. It was a book of poetry compiled from dozens of years of work.

In 2015, Andrew published "The Theft and Other Short Stories" as a collection of some of his favorite portions of his writings after he was challenged to self-publish a book. Challenged and excited about his success, he published his first novel, "Vengeful Son," in 2016 and began building a franchise with that book. "The Masterson Files" (the series containing "Vengeful Son") now includes five books and has fifteen in outline form. The story follows an ex-assassin that is reluctantly engaged in helping others while trying to retire.

In 2020, after a tragic event, Andrew co-wrote "What NOT to Say to People Who Are Grieving." This book showcased emotions and an approach to helping others be more mindful of their words during grief.

2021 gave us "A Slice of Fear" followed by "Another Slice of Fear" with short stories focusing on fears of all types. "Another Slice of Fear" won Andrew a Literary Titan Award and has been reviewed positively for several stories in the genre.

As Quality Leader and System Architect, Andrew's work gave him credit for a series of instructional manuals for site relationship management systems, various quality documents, and development lifecycles. In Andrew's spare time, he has a passion for many hobbies and his family, which he considers paramount. For more information about Andrew, please visit **andrewallensmith.com**.

Other titles available by Andrew Allen Smith:

The Masterson Files

Vengeful Son
Sinful Father
Deadly Daughter
Fateful Friend
Silent Sister
Curious Cousin

The Eternal Forever

Adam
Morgan

Slices of Fear

A Slice of Fear
Another Slice of Fear
Yet Another Slice of Fear

Non-Fiction

What NOT to say to People Who are Grieving

Other Books

A Slice of Passion
The Theft and Other Short Stories

Books containing the Work of Andrew Smith

Simple Things
A Portrait of Herbert Losch
Monster Hunter Intern
The Gift
Pages Promotions: Chaos

For more info or updated books lists visit:

andrewallensmith.com